DESCENDANCE
VOLUME 1: THE BROTHERHOOD OF THE PAST

Olscar Borcan

Descendance

Volume 1
The Brotherhood of the Past

Editions : BoD - Books on Demand
12/14 rond-point des Champs Elysées
75008 Paris
Printed by BoD - Books on Demand, Nordestedt
ISBN : 9782322240456
Legal submission: September 2020

My sincerest thanks to **Alexane PELISSOU** for the work done in the English translation of this novel.

The greatest of all accomplishments of 20th Century science
has been the discovery of human ignorance... (Thomas Lewis)

PROLOGUE

A meeting of the utmost importance was taking place in the large closed room, steeped in mortuary darkness. The people that attended represented the highest authorities of the consortium. The problematics that exposed Gaialinea, more commonly called Earth, were, until now, just a small and insignificant grain of sand on the scale of their concerns.

But that one small grain of sand was slowly turning into a rock that could, if they didn't do anything, become a boulder.

The androgynous person that was giving a speech to the consortium was called Eldmanaym. He had one and only thought : succeed in fixing the problem, where many failed before him. That success was a guarantee to access the highest position, unfilled for almost a century : the Regastral's.

— Sirs, I was just informed that we found a trace of the object stolen in the past. That object is located in the continuum Gaialinea. You all now what that object could do if it was absorbed by an individual. We cannot take that risk, even if the chances that it actually happens are tiny. For the civilisation's own good, I am asking you to vote an immediate intervention so that we can take the object back, and eliminate every person that has been in contact with it.

The twelve consuls that were part of the consortium nodded, showing their complete agreement. The confirmation, through telepathic path, validated that decision.

Despite that obvious unanimity, Krejlien, one of the twelve consuls, was in fact forced to accept that proposition even though it didn't align with his values and ideas. But right now, he couldn't take the risk to bring attention to himself.

Eldmanaym kept going with his long-winded speech :

— Since the decision is unanimous, and so we don't waste anytime, I went ahead and forestalled your agreement. I called the elite, to help us successfully complete this mission.

While he said that, the door opened, letting a dozen armed men come in.

— I personally selected the elite unit standing in front of you. These men will successfully complete this mission, I vouch for it.

The experimented men that formed the elite unit all went through an alteration of their cerebral cortex. They were now deprived of the most human function there is : compassion. In order to assure the complete devotion of these men, a small processor had been transplanted into their brain, without their consent.

Krejlien started to ask himself if accepting this proposal was the right choice to make. Maybe it would have been better to show his disagreement during the vote, hoping other consuls would join his cause ? But rumors said that this is what Eldmanaym was waiting for in order to take the power, and that he successfully passed a law that forced soldiers to go through that surgical intervention. Krejlien didn't know the pourcentage of units that had already had the surgery, but that didn't predict a bright future.

Eldmanaym took a solemn voice to address the soldiers :

— Sirs, we are all relying on you to successfully complete this mission. You will have access to our latest technologies, developed in our laboratories. You will have free rein in terms of elimination : every human that has been in contact with the crystal needs to be eliminated immediately. This crystal is vital to the balance of our civilisation, because it isn't tolerable that a group of decision-makers could betray us and put all us, as well as everything we built, at risk. The mission will start as soon as you leave this room. You may not return to the assembly without the crystal.

Every soldier put a knee to the ground, left hand in their back, right fist to the ground and raised their head to show complete obedience. They chant their motto :

— Body and spirit are one with our nation, and dying we can.

Eldmanaym made a sign with his hand, and the men got up and left the room. In his heart of hearts, he enjoyed the fact that his plan was going on smoothly, because, as for now, nothing would ever stop his rise to power.

CHAPTER I : The accident

He couldn't stop thinking about one of his recurring memories when he closed his eyes : the car getting of the road, his father turning the steering wheel far left while cursing at the boar that was standing right in the middle of a turn in Corsica. What could that animal have possibly been doing there ?

The summer holidays were coming to an end. His parents had rented, on the hills of Propriano, a gorgeous house that belonged to one of their diplomatic friends. A house that somehow escaped the national Corsican sport : bombing.

That abode had a beautiful pool, and an easy access to a gorgeous beach within a still wild inlet.

His family never got tired of watching the sunset on the Mediterranean sea everything night, after enjoying a meal cooked by their chef, and mostly made of local specialities — which was a delight for their taste bud.

They got a message the night before, asking them to get back home as soon as they could. They were now on the road back, to take an airplane at the Ajaccio airport in order to return to the continent.

He was disappointed to get back a week earlier, but those two weeks he spent with his family were amazing.

Albot was watching the road and the gully through the window. He quickly turned around to face his sister, that had just started crying and yelling after seeing that stupid beast.

The car spun around, in a way that the only direction it seemed to be taking was the void.

His father tried, as best as he could, to get back control of the vehicle, by turning the steering wheel, but in vain. The screech of tires only increased the fear that was already overwhelming.

The noise stopped all of a sudden, the same way we turn off the radio or a movie while watching it. Surprised by the silence, they all looked at each other, during a short period of time, and stayed there, frozen like statues.

Even his sister, that hadn't stopped yelling since the animal showed up, kept quiet.

The car ended up in a tree, that had been shaped by the wind. A tree leaning above a deep chasm, not far from a river they could see from the road. Half of the vehicle was standing of the tree's trunk. The other half was suspended in the void.

They thought they would get off lightly, with a huge family scare. It would be a story to tell their friends, a sort of end-of-the-holiday misadventure that ends well. The only comparison he had in mind, was when a plane slowly starts its descent, with that hydraulic pump resonating all over the cockpit to take out the landing gear. Most of the passengers imagine a catastrophic scenario, and start praying to quickly get out of that nightmare.

All of a sudden, the characteristic sound of the oil pression circuit circuit de pression d'huile was heard. Instantly, a certain smile, that showed the amount of stress they went through, appeared on their faces. A smile that was one big relief, and the translation of their gratitude because their prayers was heard. Just like the plane passengers, the intensity of their expressions said a lot about their fear. And, as if they were trying to ward off the bad luck that was striking their family, they started to smile.

As they were thinking that they miraculously escaped the Reaper, a certain serenity, and a certain joy, was floating in the vehicle.
But apparently, destiny had other gruesome projects.

The tree, that had somehow managed to grow in an unsuitable and uncomfortable place, due to the nature of the ground, slowly started to move, almost in an imperceptible way, but enough to break the balance of the delicate scale of life. It was the last thing keeping them apart from an irreversible death.

The car, pulled down by the tremor, tumbled into the void, breaking the pounding silence, reminding them of the roller-coasters from an amusement parc. With that same effect of speed and precipitation into the void.

The fall only lasted a couple of seconds. Long enough to see their life flash in front of them, just like the reel of a movie spinning way to fast. A reel made out of scenes that only you can translate, and understand.

The mother turned around, and broke the silence to tell him something he didn't quite understand :

— The chosen are the only ones who can save them. Don't ever get rid of the crystal.

His dad, who had turned around as well to smile at his sister, was now staring at him. He said, in a very serious way :

— Take good care of your sister, Albot !

His sister, who was repeatedly yelling that they were all going to die. His father who was desperately looking for something inside his pocket. His mother telling him that it was already to late.

The car touched the stony ground once, a thousand feet meters, before bouncing back like a balloon, along with the sound of strained corrugated iron, broken glass, the airbag filling itself as quick as the speed of sound, and piercing screams.
How to stay focussed ? They kept rolling towards an unavoidable death, paced by turn-overs.

His whole body was tossed around, from left to right, the drivers seat had smashed one of his legs and his head had repeatedly knocked the passengers window.
That's when he saw a sort of glow, like a flash that was suddenly lighting his pupils, before passing out after getting hurt, one last time, in the temple.

CHAPTER II : All alone

How long had he been unconscious? He didn't know. He had trouble remembering where et how he got there.

He slowly opened one eye, but he couldn't open the second one, even though he wanted to. He could only see through his right eye.

Slouched on a rock, he tried to evaluate the gravity of his wounds. Because, besides his eye, he had an unbearable pain in his right leg, and his left shoulder was facing backwards.

A warm and sweet liquid was flowing down his cheek. And he couldn't move nor emit a sound.

His attention was caught by the sound of water and babbling, and when he tried to stand despite the pain, he witnessed, completely helpless, a gory movie like scene. Their car was slowly sinking into the river, with his unconscious parents inside. He couldn't see his sister. But she was probably leaning on the back seat.

The last bits of strength left his body while he was trying to stand up and go help them, and he finally passed out… He regain consciousness, loosing once again his marks and the notion of time. The sun had now reached its zenith, meaning it was probably around noon. The pain that stroke him quickly reminded him what had happened.

Not far from him, crows were croaking in a negative way, starring at him with their red eyes, with one wish, and one wish only : devouring his family. Albot also noticed that two boars were chewing on clothes that had fallen from the car, and on a bag that must have been ejected just like him.

It was said that these animals could swallow anything, even the wheels from a car if they had to. The boy was completely helpless, incapable of moving.

The car wasn't visible anymore, it had disappeared with his one and only family inside. Tears started dropping, with an unbearable pain coming from his left eye.

He felt a beak taping on his bleeding leg, but it was impossible for him to make a sound, which could have been a great way for him to express his pain, and chase these scavengers from an Alfred Hitchcock movie. He felt weak and once again completely helpless.

He was overthinking, trying to find a solution, and ultimately get out of this mess. The voice of his mother suddenly appeared in his head. He though about all those times she told him he wouldn't be able to give him grandchildren if he kept putting his phone in the front pocket of his jeans. He asked himself whether his phone was still working, or if it was completely dead.

He finally took it of his pocket, after trying several times — which sounded like for ever. The black screen had been damaged. He pushed the « on » button, praying it would turn his phone on, and help him get out of this mess. He even made a promesse to himself if it worked : lighting up a huge altar candle.

The recognizable sound of the phone turning on immediately chased the European vultures. But was he going to be able to put his PIN number in, with only one eye and on a screen that was half broken ?

One of the boars, that was probably more that 200 pounds, showed his discontentment, loudly taping the ground with his paws, with his head forward, threatening him with his sharp tusks.

He remembered some wild boars were carnivorous. Or was it just fear that made him imagine things?

The animal stopped a yard away from his head, made a shrill sound and sniffed him. The smell of blood emanating from his wound seemed to arouse it's curiosity. The wounded man didn't know what to do, and tears of helplessness came to his eyes. Suddenly the boar turned around, because a second boar — which could have been a sow — caught its attention. He emitted a new « snout snout », then left to join the female, and disappeared into the Corsican maquis.

Albot was finally able to get back to his phone problem, because, for now, his situation was still the same. His first attempt showed a red error message, followed by a « two attempts remaining » one.

The pain became unbearable and made him sweat, increasing his fear of blocking the device. Only one more chance to get out of this ravine alive.

He had to calm down a bit to be able to type in that damn four-digit code.

From time to time, his vision got blurry. Add to that the sweat that burned one of his eyes, the only one he could still open. Typing on the tactile buttons of his phone with the hand he was using to hold it while paying attention to the number that only appeared for a few seconds was not an easy thing to do.

Miraculously, the phone turned on, with an invitation to connect himself to his telephone's operator network via an unlock code. Luckily, he had kept the original basic four-zero code.
A network bar! At the bottom of this precipice, the transmitter waves were having trouble getting through. But it was enough to make a call. Was he going to remember the emergency number? His brain was completely fogged up and softened.

That's when he had a flash. He had downloaded applications represented by large icons, one of which allowed him to call the nearest police station via his position.

He pressed the emergency call icon, put his phone on speaker, and after a few ringtones, the message that the conversation would be recorded resulted in a voice indicating that all the lines were busy, and that he could either wait or call back later.

After a few minutes, that seemed like an eternity, a female voice introduced herself, asking him for the reason of his call. In complete shock, he was totally unable to get a single syllable ouf of his mouth, and began to panic. The voice in the telephone insisted, with a « hello » that became more and more insistent.

After yet another attempt to pronounce something, he finally managed to say the only word that came to his mind: « Help! » The person on the other end of the line immediately understood the urgency of the call and asked him not to hang up so that he could be located. But with all this effort and energy, he fainted again.

When he opened his only valid eye, he saw people clustering around him like ants around a honey pot. He was on a drip, rapped in a shell, with a neck brace around his neck. He was asked questions that he was unable to understand and interpret.
Anyway, his vocal cords hurt to much for him to say anything.
He heard the sound of the helicopter above him, before he felt himself being lifted into the air. It was the last thing he grasped before he blacked out.

CHAPTER III : The awakening

After spending about four weeks in a coma, waking up in hospital was quite painful, both physically and morally. Operated and plastered, Albot was unable to feed himself and was assisted in all the most basic acts of his daily life.

Answers about his family made him fall appart. Only his parents bodies had been found. His little sister's body remained untraceable, despite several days of research in the river, by divers from the national police force.

According to the police officers, he had been incredibly lucky to have been ejected from the car when it fell off the cliff.

The most likely theory was that his seatbelt was improperly fastened, that his door opened during the impact with the ground, and that he was ejected from the vehicle in one of the many rollovers. All he could remember, and was sure of, was that his parents would never have driven a car with unfastened children. They were very careful to everything regarding the safety of their children and safety in the car was at the top of the list.

Moreover, this car was new and equipped with all the options and gadgets his father had been eager to get his hands on: front, rear and side airbags, detection of an unfastened seatbelt and an unclosed door, GPS, power steering, sunroof, puncture-proof wheel. It was the first car connected to the Internet via an on-board computer linked to the server at home.

His father had explained to his mother that it all came as a package and that there was no extra cost: that with all of these options, the children would be safe.

So it was inconceivable that his father was not alerted by the electronics on board of this four-wheeled space shuttle. Some sort of female voice would not have failed to point out unbuckled rear seat belts, just like his mother, who would have, in a firmer voice, told them to buckle their seatbelt.

Come to think of it, the car would have simply refused to start with an open door...

The boy was coping with a double fracture of the right tibia, a dislocation of the left shoulder, three cracked ribs, not to mention bruises all over his body, as well as the surgery he had for his left eye: following the impact of his skull against a tree stump, the optic nerve had been damaged.

They had managed to save his eye, but he had lost part of his vision. He felt ridiculous with his shell, which looked like an eye patch like the ones we can see in old pirate movies.

The doctors' prognosis was rather reticent and pessimistic. No one could say whether he would completely regain his sight in the medium or long term.

When he woke up, a police detective came to question him.

He had tried to explain that he had buckled his seatbelt properly and that the car would have indicated, both with an audible and a visual alarm, that a door was improperly closed. The inspector smiled nicely at him and then tried to comfort him as politely as he could. But there was nothing to be done, the words of a fourteen-year-old teenager didn't measure up to the road safety specialists and investigators seasoned by their experience on the field.

His hospital stay had stopped him from attending his parents' funeral. It was explained to him that since his sister's body had not been found, clothing and some personal items had simply been placed in the coffin.

The inspector asked many questions, but one of them was asked more insistently and formulated in different ways. The inspector wanted to know if the video recordings from the three mini-cameras — the ones in each rearview mirror filming the interior of the vehicle and the one outside filming the front and rear of the vehicle — were only stored in the vehicle's memory server.

Another one of the many gadgets in this car. To put it simply, it looked like some kind of black box, like the ones found in airplanes.

He said he didn't know for sure, but that he thought it was. His parents never, ever, mentioned a backup server at home. The young boy took the opportunity to ask if they had been able to view the videos of the accident, but they hadn't. All the data was corrupted and unrecoverable. Albot was about to say something, but his mouth remained shut. What's the point of arguing? Some things were unclear and he had no desire to give additional information to a complete stranger, even if this complete stranger was a police inspector.

Before leaving, he handed over his business card and told him to contact him in case his memory came back. He grumbled a small inaudible « yes » before the police officer walked out the door.

Despite all the drugs he was on, he was still hurting like hell. The only thing that partly allowed him to forget his pain was to think about his sister and his parents: grief was taking over the pain .

He was transferred from the Timone hospital in Marseille to the Berck-sur-Mer hospital in the north of France — which specializes in the disabled — for two months of rehabilitation. Two long months of reeducation, but also psychological reconstruction. His morale was low. He had two reeducation sessions a day, one in the morning and one in the afternoon, with a psychotherapy session in between.

The hospital, located in front of the sea, allowed him to take long invigorating walks in a wheelchair. What could be better than the salty air to give him strength, and the sound of the ocean to relax him?

The therapist tried to give him a taste of life, but it was not an easy task. To admit what had happened, was to admit the lost of his only family.

He couldn't help but imagine his parents and his little sister walking through the door of his hospital room, bringing him his favorite milk chocolates with praline filling. The smell of chocolate made him drool just thinking about it.

Since he was underaged, this time spent in Berck allowed the doctors to find a solution for his custody. His parents were orphans, so he had no relatives to take care of him. He was unable to move, but his parents' lawyer took care of everything, and spent a whole day in the hospital reading him the testamentary letter.

Their wish was that their children would be placed in the Descendance Orphanage in case they disappeared, and nowhere else. This place had great significance : they had grown up there and met each other there. Proof that life is an eternal beginning...

The lawyer also gave him a kind of tube with the inscription « to the attention of my children, Albot and Catiana Coldi ».

— What is it, he asked the lawyer.

— I have no idea. When I asked your father the same question, he told me that I didn't need to know, that I should only give it to you in case he passed away.

He placed the tube in the hanging drawer on the left side of his bed, thinking that he would look at it peacefully later. But this object had aroused his curiosity.

His parents owned shares in a number of companies around the world. He particularly remembered a company in the microtechnology field, in which they were the sole shareholders.

Their life insurance and all their assets were enough savings for him to be able to do great studies and start his life serenely.

What intrigued him was that his parents had also stipulated in bold letters in their will that under no circumstances, and under no conditions, should the family home be sold without the consent of the last descendant. He could make this decision not when he arrived at the age of majority, but on the date of his twenty-one year old birthday. In the event of the premature death of the parents, the children must absolutely keep the house in their possession at any cost.

It seemed rather odd, as this house was not a family property that would have been handed down from generation to generation. It was a rather modern house, with an avant-garde and innovative architecture, also referred as intelligent, communicating and autonomous. His father had it built, after designing it himself ten years earlier.

Another clause stipulated that part of the inheritance would remain blocked for the inside and the outside maintenance of the house, but also to pay current bills.

Albot could only take possession of his property when he came of age, but until then he had to live at the Descendance Orphanage.

He cherished the sweet hope that a caring family would be willing to take him, but since he was fourteen, it was unlikely that would ever happen.

As soon as his lawyer walked away, he immediately went to the computer that was on self-service at the entrance of the hospital. He wanted to get all the information he needed for his detention. Because in his mind, this could not be compared with anything other than a prison.

But no matter how many hours he spent surfing, no search engine was able to find any information that could help him, except that it was an orphanage.

He was not fully recovered, and was still unable to use a wheelchair. But he made small progress every day, that gave him courage and hope. One evening, a doctor came to his room to tell him that he could be out before the end of the week. He said that a nurse would come in the evening to explain the exercises he would have to keep doing at home for his rehabilitation.

He would have liked, indeed, to practice these exercises at home. But he didn't know what his new home would look like.

The day before he was discharged from hospital, a lady in her forties came to visit, and introduce herself. It was Mrs. Helena Foxter, who was a member of the board of directors of the Descendance Orphanage. She informed him that she knew his parents very well and hoped that he would blossom in the pleasant living environment within the Descendance community.

She understood the difficulties he had projecting himself so quickly into his new environment, but he needed to take back control of his life.

His parents were planning to take him to the Descendance Orphanage this year, to show him the place where they had grown up. But the turn of events had made this visit permanent.

Mrs. Foxter explained to him that a driver would pick him up the next day, late in the morning, and that he would drive him home to pick up a few things before leaving that evening for the orphanage.

All that was needed was the bare minimum, just enough to settle in: one suitcase would be enough. The orphanage provided clothing and toiletries.

She handed him her business card, emphasizing that he could call her day or night and that he should not forget that the Descendance was now his only family.

Once she left, he stood there for a while, reflecting on everything. What could that cylindrical object be? After making sure that he would not be disturbed anymore, he opened the drawer of his bedside table to take the strange object in his hands, and began to examine it.

CHAPTER IV : The cylinder

The cylinder was anthracite, and was about ten inches long and two inches wide. The material of which it was made out of was somewhat odd and seemed quite light. But what bothered him the most was that he couldn't see how to open it. Because there were absolutely no marks at the ends to remove or unscrew any kind of lid.

It was nearly 11 P.M., and the nurse was going to do her nightly rounds and come by to check on him. He put the cylinder under his pillow and laid down, pretending to be asleep. The nurse arrived a few moments later, with another person.

She checked that he was asleep, and the man began to look in his bedside table, under his bed, in the small cupboard where his clothes were, and finally in the bathroom. He seemed upset because he couldn't find what he was looking for.

Albot decided to wake up and ask them what they were looking for, but he changed his mind at the last minute: a little alert in his head told him not to do anything about it.

The nurse and her companion eventually left the room. The boy managed to catch a glimpse of the man for only a few seconds, just before the nurse closed the door. He was in his thirties. He was dressed in a black suit and tie, had blond hair and was at least five feet tall. The man looked rather unhappy, because when he left the room, Albot heard something that made him panic: the man intended to look at the recordings from the camera in his room as soon as the security post opened. He intended to find out where the object was hidden.

Albot waited a good ten minutes before sitting on his bed laying on the wall. He thought about what he had just witnessed, and a thousand questions were piercing through his brain. Who was that man? Where was this camera, supposed to be filming him? Why did they put one in his room?

More importantly, why did the man want the object his father had left him? So many questions that could be answered with the cylinder he had just taken out from under his pillow and was now holding in his hands.

He had been looking at the object from every angle for over an hour, but he didn't notice anything. Not the slightest gap, hidden button or mechanism. All he could see was this sentence engraved on the cylinder: « To my children Albot and Catiana Coldi ». He had said the sentence without realizing that he was reading it out loud and not in his head.

An imperceptible little click caught his attention... This click would have gone completely unnoticed in other circumstances and other places. But the room was plunged into a monastery silence, where the slightest mosquito noise would have been immediately perceived as a thunderclap.

The cylinder showed a gap of a few inches along its entire length. A translucent sheet appeared through the gap, that was about six inches high. After a few moments, Albot saw a square, a round and a triangle appear.

First the triangle turned blue, then after a few seconds it turned red and finally green. The circle became blue and a logo in the shape of a fingerprint appeared. Instinctively, he positioned his right thumb on the screen, and the circle also became green.

That's when the image of his father appeared on the square of the screen:

— Good morning, children. If you are reading this message, it means that your mother and I are no longer of this world.

First of all, we wanted to say that we are sincerely sorry for having left you orphans. We hope that our friends from the Descendance will be able to give you all the help and love that we can no longer give you. You can have blind faith in these people, for they are all trustworthy and they will be able to accompany you until you come of age.

This security device has detected that the room you're in is being monitored. But if the circle went through the color red and then green, it means that this object managed to interfere with all the surveillance system that could have been close to you. I know it sounds a bit James Bondy, but the end will be more like *Mission : Impossible*, because this message will self-destruct and cannot be listened to twice.

His father winked at him:

— I'm going to entrust you with something and an object that you must never part with. First of all, you must go home and go to my office. You don't have the keys to get in, but Albot knows the way to my room. You have to use the laptop on my desk with the crystal nearby.

Put the crystal in the gap on the right side of the laptop, follow the instructions on the computer and you will see the bookcase sink into the wall, leaving room for an entrance that goes down into my lab in the basement.

Once downstairs, you will find, in a blue transparent cube, a second hanging crystal. Take it, and do not part with it under any circumstances until you have reached the Descendance.

When you get there, tell Mr. Ziegler, the director of the orphanage, the whole story. He will then explain to you in greater detail what that crystal represents.

One last thing: there is a good chance that ill-intentioned people will try to retrieve this crystal, which contains space-time coordinates, allowing access to other worlds. My work on this object is not finished, and it may contain other functions or properties that I haven't had time to discover.

Surely you must have questions about that crystal, and might be wondering if your poor father hasn't gone a little crazy? It would be a little too long and complicated for me to explain the story behind this object. But you should know that if this crystal were to fall into the wrong hands, it could be catastrophic. It could be the key that would open Pandora's box, bringing chaos and desolation for humanity.

Just know one thing, the Einstein-Rosen bridge must never be opened for certain people.

As I told you, this message will self-destruct. Know that your mother and I love you from the bottom of our hearts.

Tears came to Albot's eyes, and he couldn't hold them back. The sheet went into the cylinder, the gap disappeared, and a small noise, which lasted two seconds, was heard, meaning that the message had self-destructed — and without any smoke.

He put the cylinder in his bedroom drawer, as it was no longer of any use. His visitor could now find it and take it, he didn't care about it. It might even save him time.

It was almost two in the morning, and Albot couldn't see how he would manage to fall asleep, since he was super excited. Sentences and words were going round and round in his head: crystal, Einstein-Rosen bridge, passage, Descendance, Pandora's box...
But eventually, fatigue got the better of him.

He woke up quite late in the morning, surprised that the nurse did not wake him up much earlier, as she usual does. But he had a foreboding and quickly opened the bedside drawer to find that the cylinder had disappeared.
He had to pretend that the cylinder was no longer in its place, otherwise people who were after him would be suspicious of its real usefulness. He rang to call a nurse, and began to address her in a rather unpleasant tone, complaining that the object was missing.
It was inadmissible for someone to break into his room in the middle of the night to steal it. He said it was the last gift he got from his parents, and the tremolos of his voice allowed him to strike the poor nurse.
She had just started her shift, and had probably nothing to do with this theft. But the comedy he had to play had to appear realistic and plausible. The night nurse ended her shift at eight in the morning and the security post opened at seven. Albot assumed that his visitor had been able to view the films in less than an hour, had found the footage he was looking for and had used the nurse one last time before her shift ended. The object had therefore been stolen by 8 A.M. at the latest.
He must be careful not to communicate his suspicions to the nurse who stood in front of him and who, armed with patience, kept apologizing. She did not understand how this was possible, and claimed that there had never been any theft in the hospital, that she would report the incident to the manager, and that he would surely be compensated for his loss. If he had been filmed, they would get their money's worth, and he would surely get a little Oscar.

CHAPTER V: Home sweet Home

The driver arrived the day after the object was stolen at eleven o'clock sharp. The doctor signed him out and the driver picked him up.

— Hello. You can call me Gustave. I'm here to take you home and then we'll take the plane to the orphanage.

— I'm Albot.

The limousine ride took almost three hours. The passenger had tried to stay awake, but without much success. The cortisone medication put him into a coma.

When he woke up, he recognized the city they were passing through, not without a touch of nostalgia. They were only a few minutes away from his house. Gustav suggested, if he wanted to, to have lunch in a fast-food restaurant nearby before they reached their destination. He accepted the offer, because the food at the hospital was awful, and once he will get to the orphanage, he wouldn't have the chance to eat a hamburger anytime soon... Despite the constant criticism of junkfood, the quality of the products and the way the fast food chains distributed them, he couldn't help but like it.

After placing the order, Gustave let him go and sit down, because with his crutches he wasn't much use for carrying the trays.

The meal unfolded in a silence interspersed with chewing noises. You could hear the flies. In the middle of the meal, Gustav asked him if he was feeling well. And after he nodded, he didn't open his mouth again.

At the end of the meal, Gustav tried to relax the atmosphere:

— Did you know that I knew your parents? They were very much in love.

— How did you know them?

— They used to come to the orphanage regularly, and sometimes I would take them there.

— I didn't know they kept visiting the orphanage.

— They were honorary members because as donors and former residents they had some privileges.

— What kind of privileges?

— Look, I shouldn't have told you about your parents. I'm sorry, I'll ask you not to tell the administrator.

— You haven't said anything derogatory or shocking to me. I don't understand your embarrassment.

Silence was his only answer. But Albot didn't insist. At the end of the meal, he asked Gustave for a small favor:

— Can we make a small detour, please?

— I've been asked to take you straight to your house. I have already broken the law by taking you to lunch at a fast-food restaurant... I'm liable to get a slap on the wrist.

— Let's not exaggerate, we just stopped for lunch for an hour. There's nothing extraordinary about that!

— Where would you like to go?

— Downtown. I'd like to buy some chocolates. There's a boutique there, and I can't even begin to tell you how happy I am when their chocolates melt in my mouth. You'll tell me what you think. I've been dreaming about them for weeks, and my parents used to buy them for us all the time.

The driver had a hard time not giving in. After all the hardships this young man had gone through, he could hardly see himself refusing.

— All right, but make it quick. Mrs. Foxter is going to call me soon, and I don't want to end up babbling excuses or lying to her.

— It'll take about 15 minutes at the most. And you won't regret it, trust me.

Once in front of the store, there was no place to park.

— What do we do now?

— You wait for me here, and...

— I'll stop you right there, you're not going out without me. I'll put on the hazard lights on and double-park. I'm coming with you.

When they entered the store, they were overwhelmed by the scents and smells released from the chocolate boxes.

Albot's brain immediately sent a message to his subconscious, to bring back to his mind the last time he had enjoyed these chocolates with his family.

It must have shown on his face, because Gustave and the saleswoman were staring at him without saying a word.

— Uh, hello, Mrs. Derby, could you please make me an assortment box, as usual?

— Hello, my little Albot, yes, right away. In the meantime, help yourself with the chocolates that are in the little basket at the cash desk, it will make you wait. But first I'd like to tell you that I was very saddened by what happened to you and your family. My sincere condolences. Here's an assortment just the way you like it.

— How much do I owe you?

Gustave was about to take out his wallet to pay, when Mrs. Derby put her hand on his arm:

— Albot, I can't take a penny from you for that box of chocolates. It's not much, but let me give it to you, hoping it will bring you some comfort.

— I don't know what to tell you. Thank you, Mrs. Derby.

She laid a kiss on his forehead, and a tear, that she didn't have time to hold back, flew down her cheek.

— I'll walk you to the door.

Gustave and Albot were about to leave when Albot saw two municipal police officers around the sedan. They were writing a ticket for parking inconvenience.

— Is this your car, sir?

— Uh, yes. I stopped for a few minutes to get some chocolates and...

— Yeah, yeah, it's always the same lame excuses. You're in breach. You're double-parked.

Mrs. Derby stormed out of her store like a crazy person.

— Listen to me, big boy, she said, addressing the youngest police officer, I think this kid has had enough. You tear up this paper, or I'll tell your mother.

The young policeman turned red. He had known Ms. Derby all his life, and his mother was one of his best friends.

— But, Mrs. Derby, I'm just doing my job.

— And you owe your job to that boy's father. Otherwise, you'd be in a detention center or something.

The young policeman's colleague recognized Albot.

— Don't insist, just leave it. We'll replace the ticket with a chocolate.

Albot handed him the box he had in his hands.

— No, not yours, kid, but Mrs. Derby is going to offer us a praline chocolate.

The shopkeeper smiled with all her white teeth.

— Come, both of you, I'll give you a little box of my best chocolates. And you, Albot, if you need anything, you can always count on me. I wish you a nice day.

— Thank you, Mrs. Derby, and thank you, sir.

The policeman gave him a friendly wave as he touched his hat, and walked back to the chocolate shop.

Gustave opened the right rear door for Albot. He entered the sedan, not without noticing the sadness on the faces of the people on the sidewalk. People who must surely have been aware of his tragic story, which they had read about in the newspapers or seen on television like any other news flash.

It took them about 15 minutes to get to their destination.

But once they got in front of the house, Gustave asked him for the key.

— I don't have a key!

— How do we get in, then?

— We don't need one.

Albot brought his finger to the door and heard the rattling of the locks.

Electronic lock by fingerprint. And a facial recognition camera replaced the peephole.

— Well, your father was ahead of his time!

— Yes, he was.

They entered, and the entrance light came on automatically.

A female voice was then heard.

— Hello, Mr. Albot. You have several messages in your mailbox and on the answering machine. Your parents and your sister are not with you?

— Hello, Lucile. No, my parents and sister aren't with me. I'll explain later.

— Is the person accompanying you allowed to be here?

— Yes, don't worry, Lucile.

— Could you give me the password, please?

— *Metadremos*.

— Correct password, Mr. Albot.

— Put yourself on standby for now.

— Very well, Mr. Albot.

— And who's that?, Gustave asked.

— Just the computer that runs the house. It's not Stark's computer, but my dad worked on it. He was working on a new concept. He used to say that it was going to revolutionize the world. But my dad was a big, sweet dreamer, according to my mom.

— Your father was a brilliant scientist, I'll tell you that.

Albot wondered how Gustave could be so assertive about his father. But he would understand sooner than later.

— Come into the kitchen, to have a cold drink or a coffee.

— I wouldn't mind a cup of coffee.

— And let's open this box of chocolates, so I can give you a taste of these wonders.

He handed the box to Gustave, who hesitated to make a choice.

— Take this one, it's my favorite, and tell me what you think.

— Indeed, the detour was worth it.

They stood there for a few minutes, enjoying the chocolates. But time passed, and the day was slowly coming to an end. Gustave gave him a few hours to pack his suitcase, and asked permission to sit on the dining room couch while he waited for him. And he began to channel-hop on the satellite, connected to the Oled screen.

CHAPTER VI: Descent History

Albot somehow went up to his room with his crutches. His first instinct was to turn on his laptop and check his e-mails. He started by going through the various emails he received from his friends, who wished him a good recovery and offered him various tributes and condolences following the disappearance of his parents and sister.

His attention was caught by a spam-like email that had arrived on his email account. He was about to delete it, but the title made him curious: « Descendance History ». The email contained an attached file. There was no sender and no date in the header, which seemed very odd.

The old medieval castle, bequeathed at the end of the 19th century to a cardinal by a rich owner without descendants, was intended to be transformed into a convent. But the virulence of the Spanish flu that hit the country in 1918, decimating entire cities and causing millions of deaths around the world, changed the fate of this donation.

The village church was saturated with sick people and their young children who were dying of lack of care from their parents. These children were crying their eyes out because they did not understand the reasons for this abandonment, this loss of protection. These bodies lying on the ground in the middle of winter barely had the spark of life to drag themselves to the toilet, and their parents were too busy trying to escape from the Reaper, who would take these dying people away in their sleep.

This pandemic left many orphans on our doorsteps, as the flu mainly affected young adults, young fathers or mothers.

The castle was quite naturally transformed into an orphanage, in order to cope with the emergencies of the moment. The news quickly spread, and soon hundreds of children arrived from all over the area and even from Paris. The archbishopric was quickly overwhelmed by all these children, and the Sisters of Holy Mercy were quickly sent there to help these poor children.

Not all of them survived. Their bodies were either burned or buried in the mass grave, blessed by a shovelful of lime that was thrown on them. The contamination was at its peak when, as if by some miracle, the disease stopped dead in the castle. No more deaths, no more contaminations, while Death continued to knock on people's doors. But no longer in the castle...

The sisters of the archdiocese were themselves very surprised by these unexpected recoveries, and they decided not to say anything, scared that it would bring more children. For there was still a big problem: Jesus didn't cook the bread, so how were they going to feed these little mouths?

Since one miracle never comes alone, they were surprised one morning to discover one of the rooms of the castle filled with an abundance of food of all kinds. But what caught their attention, apart from the food — which they didn't really feel confident about— was the materials everything was wrapped around, a kind of colored resin, extensible and very resistant.

Once the food was taken out of the wrappers, the envelopes degraded visibly until they disappeared overnight. Even though this food was out of the ordinary, the nuns were forced to use it or else the children would die of starvation. They decided to taste it first, to make sure it was edible and not dangerous. They waited two days before distributing it.

The packing slips that accompanied the boxes were very accurate about everything that was in them, with symbols in front of each line indicating what they could be used for.

The people who had placed all this food in this room had even gone through the trouble of providing some indications on the use of certain ingredients, which at first glance felt very strange.

The castle closed its doors, because the sisters did not want the word to get out there. The parish priest continued to bring back a few children who were in poor health and dying. But each time the same phenomenon occurred : the child recovered within a few days without any plausible explanation, because no medicine or treatment had been given to him.

At the end of the epidemic, some of the surviving parents came to recover their children, but the percentage remained low. More than three hundred children remained at Sainte-Descendance (as the orphanage was then called).

The pope at the time even made a quick appearance to bless the castle, but was unable to give a coherent explanation of the past events. He ordered the room where the food had appeared to be closed : the two access doors were sealed. And he ordered that no one should ever talk about what had happened, because he did not want it to become a new place of pilgrimage. No apparition or miracle had taken place, and without any proof, he did not want the matter to get out and this castle to become a new holy place.

Time passed as peacefully as possible in the castle, and the clergy scattered all the witnesses of the phenomenon all around the world.

***

The story could have ended there, but a new major event took place, this time around the middle of World War Two — which brought Saint-Descendance into the limelight, giving it a new lease of life.

An SS regiment of the German army decided to set up its headquarters in the castle. When they discovered that some of the children were Jewish, they decided to do something about it :

First, the SS decided to shoot some of the nuns who refused to help with designating the Jewish children from the non-Jewish ones. When these executions failed to change the minds of the others, the children were locked in the basement of the castle with the nuns and employees. After feeding them water and stale bread for several days, they decided to kill everyone!

One of the German officers, who refused to take part in the carnage, was beaten to death and locked in the basement with them. When he came back to his senses, he told them what his former comrades intended to do with them, and he began to cry, asking for forgiveness. There was a silence of resignation. Distress and helplessness could be seen on their faces, since they were shocked by the monstrosity of these men.

How could anyone kill in cold blood, for no reason at all, over two hundred children? Especially since those butchers had planned to set the castle on fire and make it look like an accident...

Prayers were said throughout the day until the evening. The officer explained how his former comrades intended to kill them : by sending gas through the air ducts while they slept, preventing them from sleeping through the night.

A calm and peaceful atmosphere had settled in. Everyone was resigned to die. At dawn, everyone was surprised to still be of this world. They though that this it must have been part of the Germans' diabolical plan, and that it was only a postponement: it would probably be for the next night.

This was a new torment that reinforced the cruelty of their executioners: they would have to wait for death once again, just like those prisoners on the death row, who keep waiting for their execution.

The day passed, and no meal was brought to them. Their executioners surely must have thought that it was useless to spend food on those who were going to die. The children were crying from hunger, but no matter how many hours they pounded at the door and shouted for mercy, no one came to bring anything.

In the early morning, they were again amazed to be alive. And soon, the most far-fetched theories were put forward, ranging from a last burst of humanity among the torturers to the fear of being condemned to die of hunger.

In the early afternoon, they heard footsteps : someone was in the staircase leading to the basement. Everyone's heart was pounding, but they were resigned. They preferred a quick death, by being shot, rather than having to endure the agonizing death of these poor children without being able to do anything about it.

The big wooden door opened, making squeaking sounds and plunging the entire audience into silence. Once the door was open, a woman dressed all in black appeared on the threshold, a rather tall and slender silhouette, with magnificent blond hair pulled back and eyes as blue as the sky. She looked like a demon coming from hell, to lead them to their final resting place. Or did they simply die in their sleep?

They all froze, not knowing what to do nor say. The young woman looked at all of them, one after the other, without saying a word. She turned around and disappeared up the stairs, leaving the door wide open behind her. Those who were still lying or sitting got up, and everyone looked at each other, wondering what to do. They walked slowly towards the door, expecting at any moment to see soldiers coming down the stairs and shooting at every moving soul.

A first child walked through the door, so casually it almost felt like the door had always been open and he had just come down five minutes earlier to fetch a bottle from the cellar. The German soldier who had been imprisoned with them took the lead, grabbed the child in his arms, turned around and indicated everyone to follow him. He went up a first step, then, after hesitating for a minute, a second one. He began to climb the rest of the steps slowly, as the hesitation faded away. Halfway up, he turned around and saw that everyone was behind him, following his lead. He felt responsible : he had to get these people out of there as quickly as possible, before his former comrades started shooting at them.

He felt disgusted thinking about those soldiers who could no longer act with reason, and who were ready to kill children, civilians and representatives of God, for the sole glory of a madman. He refused to take part in these murders, to stand there and do nothing about it; he would rather die with these poor people than continue to live all his life with the weight of their death on his conscience. How could he possibly justify this sordid massacre before God, or anyone else?

He was not a true Catholic, even though that's the impression he might give : he did not go to church every Sunday, and had never made a confession. But his status as a human being made him capable of judging the rightness of his choices and actions. No human being should be allowed to do such despicable things to his fellows. What set him apart from animals was his awareness of his actions. Nothing in the world can justify acts of barbarism towards fellow human beings, or even towards animals.

He soon arrived at the doorway that lead to the cursive. His heart was racing, ready to explode at any moment. He delicately put the child he was holding in his arms down, kissed him on the forehead and indicated him to go back with the others, placing his finger on his lips to show him that he couldn't make any sound. He then held his hand in front of him, with his fingers spread out, to show them that they mustn't go any further.

He gently opened the door. The hinges made an inaudible creaking sound. He felt that, from the bottom of his soul, his senses were on alert and amplified. He could almost hear the child's heartbeat.

He opened the door a few inches. He got blinded by the light for a moment, and had to wait a few seconds to get used to the daylight again. Once he was able to distinguish something other than shapes again, he noticed that there was no activity outside. There was a morbid silence and an absence of abnormal activity, even though it was the middle of the day. After an hour of looking around, he had to face the fact that there were no living souls, except for the people who had come up with him from the basement.

Was there a catch? The SS Colonel in command of this base had a reputation for sordid behavior. This colonel was unbalanced enough to do this sort of thing. Stories were being told about him. One of the most sordid stories, among many others, took place during a hunting party in the Black Forest. At the end of the game, he thought that the animals he had just hunted down had been too easily killed. He ordered his corporal to bring him three soldiers from his regiment, randomly picked out. The three soldiers were then selected and brought to him. After taking their weapons from them, he told them that he was giving them a two-minute head start.

Their first reflex was to believe that it was a bad joke, or some sort of training session. They quickly changed their minds when the Colonel pointed the barrel of his Walther P38 on the forehead of one of the soldiers, pulled the trigger and sprayed the other two with blood and pieces of brain. The lieutenant who had witnessed the scene started vomiting, and the colonel ordered him to surrender his weapon and replace the soldier laying at his feet.

For two of these men, the nightmare stopped quite quickly. But the last one, who was the lieutenant, managed to stay alive until nightfall. Which made the colonel mad as hell! His lieutenant was still alive! He refused to be ridiculed in front of the other officers, and he realized that he was facing a dilemma. Pardoning his former officer would make him lose his authority.

He yelled into the forest to let the lieutenant know that the hunt was over and that he could return. The officer came out of a grove, injured by branches and thorns. The colonel waited until he was two yards away from him, gave him a Hitler salute with his left hand, which was immediately returned to him by his lieutenant. But with his right hand, he shot him in the chest, which immediately caused him to collapse on the ground. He then approached his dying victim, to end his suffering by placing another bullet through his heart. He then bent down to close his eyes, whispering in his ear : « I can't stand the smell of vomit! » The witnesses of the event remained impassive, and the fear in their eyes reassured the colonel of the soundness of his decision. Back at the camp, he turned to his major and said: « All this has whetted my appetite! »

The soldier walked into the cursive, without seeing a living soul. The vehicles were all lined up in the courtyard, but there was not the slightest suspicious noise or movement. To get it over with, he decided to go and stand in the middle of the courtyard. He turned around once, then a second and a third time, making sure to look at every building, every roof, every dark spot to see if there was any movement. But not the slightest movement could be noticed: he had to admit that there was no one left. As a security measure, he decided to visit a few buildings to make sure and assure those who were waiting for his return that they were no longer in danger.

He found a gun on a table, checked that it was loaded and took it with him on his visits. Those minutes must have lasted an eternity for those who were still on the stairs or still waiting in the basement. But he had to check everything. He didn't want to see that butcher, the colonel, show up when they released themselves.

While inspecting the various buildings, he found weapons in their cases, and the packages the soldiers lined up at the end of their beds. The kitchens were also empty, tidy and clean. There was not a single shell casing on the floor that would have indicated that a fight had taken place within these walls. Nothing was broken or damaged, the lights were all off, as were the radio transmitters. The German pressed the button to turn on one of the devices, but nothing happened. Same with the light switches.

The drawbridge was still raised and the gate was down. How could they have left the castle without raising the gate and lowering the drawbridge? This fortified castle was surrounded by a several yards ditch filled with water, making it almost impossible to cross. Perhaps they had found a secret passage? He decided to postpone his reflections to later, because the children were starting to get impatient.

When he opened the door, the sunbeam immediately entered the staircase, blinding the first children, the same way it had blinded him earlier. The children were siting on the steps, waiting patiently for him to come and deliver them. He waved at them, showing that they could follow him, that there was no more danger.

They were all now in the yard, and not a word had been said. The silence remained as if they were afraid to wake up the soldiers and see them show up with their machine guns slung over their shoulders. The first sentence that emerged from the group was one spoken by the same child who had gone first through the door: « I am hungry… »

After reading this email, Albot felt puzzled. Why would someone send him this, and who knew that he had to go to the Descendance?

CHAPTER VII: The Crystal

That e-mail had him stumped and confused. A certain nostalgia, which seemed to come from a distant past, overwhelmed him. He had only been away for three months, but it seemed like an eternity. He took a suitcase from under his bed and his things from his wardrobe and laid it on his bed. He didn't know what to take. His mother used to pack for them, when they would go on a holiday. He now felt a bit lost. This memory of his mother brought tears to his eyes, tears that ran down his cheeks.

While he was trying to pack his clothes in the suitcase, he remembered a discussion that occurred a few months earlier at the diner table.

His father said that if something happened to their family, it was absolutely necessary to retrieve the documents and objects that were locked in his office, and in the second room... He didn't have time to finish his sentence, because his mother had stopped the discussion altogether, saying that it was too early to talk about it, that he and his sister were too young to understand. Their father hadn't insisted, because of the look his mom had gave him. Who would have done otherwise, by the way?

He knew he wouldn't have the opportunity to return to his house anytime soon, and his curiosity about these documents and objects was amplified by all the events that had taken place recently.

His parents' bedroom, which was at the end of the hallway, had a private staircase leading directly to his father's office on the ground floor. His father had installed this second access so that he wouldn't wake up the whole house when he worked late. Albot decided to go there, as his father had asked him to, without using the main staircase, because he did not want to justify nor explain anything to Gustav.

From the top of the stairs, he informed the driver that he was going to rest in his room for a while before leaving, because he was tired from the journey.

Gustave was so absorbed in his movie that he didn't ask any question. He simply said « OK ». But Albot was convinced that he would soon go up and check on him, probably within the next 30 minutes.

The half hour was shortened to fifteen minutes. Gustav tiptoed up, and checked on the teenager to make sure he was sleeping soundly.

As soon as he heard the sound coming from the television again, indicating that Gustave had resumed watching his movie, he got up and began walking down the second staircase. He walked slowly to his parents' room at the end of the hallway, which lead to the four bedrooms and washrooms on the first floor. He tried to make as little noise as possible in the hallway, but it's wasn't easy because of his crutches.

When he arrived at the door, he paused to make sure that the sound of the TV was still audible. He gently opened the door and entered the room. The pictures of his parents and sister, neatly placed on the chest of drawers, as well as on the walls, brought tears to his eyes. He had to pull himself together quickly, for this was neither the time nor the place to feel sorry for himself.

After wiping his tears with his shirt's sleeves, he walked to the closet door that was the second entrance to his father's office. He remembered the time his father first showed him this passage. He was just seven years old. His father had led him to believe it was a secret passageway. And it was true that you had to have a keen eye to detect its entrance, and its spiral staircase. This one was quite steep. Luckily, his father had had a handrail installed along the wall, so that he could be sure to catch it when he came down. When he reached the bottom, he faced a door, which seemed rather heavy and difficult to open. But once in the room, he understood why. The door was made out of shelves full of books that weighed it down.

The office was the size of two rooms on the first floor, probably around 430 square feet. The floor was made out of wood, there was a large desk with a laptop facing the central door, a flat screen on the wall, a large bookcase with a large sofa and a coffee table. Not to mention the espresso machine that his father could no longer live without. Walls were covered with family photos and paintings. At first, he didn't notice anything special.

He came down to carry out his father's last wishes, and now curiosity dominated his mind. The first chest, which was located behind the flat screen on the wall, had been emptied. The lawyer must have already came here. He recognized the glass-looking paperweight that his father had described to him on the desk. It had a rectangular shape, was about three by two inches, the contours were bevelled and less than two inches thick. He expected the object to carry a certain weight, but when he took it in his hands, it felt like he was holding a feather.

The last word his father had said before he disappeared, « crystal », immediately came to his mind. He had to quickly return to his room before he caught the attention of his driver. He noticed his father's second laptop on the desk.
The second, because the first one was in the car with them when they had the accident. It was a new generation computer, much better than the one he had in his room. He opened it, and it turned on automatically:
— Hello, Coldi! How can I help you, asked a voice coming from the device.
Albot didn't want to waste any time and went straight to the point. He noticed the slot on the right side of the computer, which looked nothing like a memory card reader or some old discs that his father took great pleasure in showing and describing to him to make him understand how quickly technology had evolved. It had more to do with the size of the crystal on the desk. He took it and placed it in front of the hole that had a sort of small flap to prevent dust from getting inside the device. And then, with a sharp jerk, he inserted the crystal into the computer.
The computer's display immediately changed to show a logo, a sort of tree in a triangle, he did not recognize. He heard a new message:
— Please place your thumb on the fingerprint reader.
Albot recognized the fingerprint reader in the lower right corner of the laptop keyboard. He placed his thumb on it. He surprisingly felt a slight tingling sensation on his finger. He looked at it and noticed a tiny drop of blood.

No computer in the world, no matter how powerful, could read a DNA code in a second. However, three rectangles appeared on the screen with a green acronym in the foreground. The first one showed his photo, the second one his fingerprint and the third one a DNA symbol. The computer confirmed the authorization.

— Access authorization confirmed, you may now enter.

— But where?

A shelf full of books, on the opposite side of the room, sank into the wall in a silence he could not have imagined, and the wooden floor collapsed into a staircase that immediately lit up. This was the entrance to the lower room. Albot hobbled towards it, and immediately began his descent. He came down somehow, and discovered, downstairs, some sort of laboratory, much larger than the office upstairs. It was filled with measuring devices, computers, and things he had never seen before. The room must have been about a thousand square feet, had several windows that were flat screens showing a seaside landscape. His father had probably installed them to avoid becoming claustrophobic.

He moved from one workbench to another, trying to imagine what his father could do in a place like this. He suddenly remembered why he was here. The crystal!

He noticed the transparent box, lightened in blue, which his father had described to him in his message. He walked towards it and didn't see anything inside. He was about to panic when, as he was looking away, he noticed a slight shift coming from inside the box. He opened it and discovered the crystal, floating in the air. He took it out of the box to examine it more closely: it looked exactly like the crystal on his father's desk.

He decided to follow his father's instructions anyway. He didn't quite understand what the crystal would do for him, but he decided to put it in his pocket. And he walked up the stairs back to his father's office. The stairs disappeared immediately under the bookcase when Albot removed the first crystal from the computer.

He had completely forgotten to take his personal computer with him, in order to replace the one he was about to take. He had to go back to his room. It wasn't going to be easy since he still had to carry his crutches around. He gathered his courage, and began the obstacle course. He only took one crutch and used his second arm, which was free, to carry the computer.

He finally got to his room, sweating. He quickly put the laptop in his suitcase, under his clothes. And after catching his breath, he made his way back to the office, with his own computer. This time, he put it into a backpack he found in his room, to carry it easily.

After minutes that seemed like hours, he sat down on the desk chair to catch his breath. He got up and was about to leave, when he changed his mind and looked again at the first crystal he had left on the desk. He noticed a silkscreen print inside the crystal. He took it in his hands and raised it to the window to see if, hoping the light of the sun would help. But he could not read what was written. It was the same logo than the that had appeared on his computer.

He put the first crystal on the desk and took the one that was in the lab out of his pocket: he wanted to check if it had the same logo. But as soon as the first ray of sunlight hit the crystal, a violet ray came out from the opposite side. This ray hit not only his valid eye, but also the one with the eye patch, which made him stagger. Because he was surprised, and in a lot of pain, the crystal fell out of his hands...

He had the impression that the crystal was falling in slow motion on the floor, he could already see it explode into thousands of pieces in a din that would alert Gustav, but against all expectations, when it reached the floor, it didn't make a sound. Not the slightest splinter came out of it. It had not bounced or moved from where it had fallen. It was as if it had fallen on a down pillow.

Albot was speechless, and looked at the crystal on the ground, without picking it up, as if it might bite him if he touched it. He was starting to think clearly again when he heard footsteps coming from the corridor and approaching the office. He had wasted too much time going back and forth.

Why did he feel the need to hide ? He was home! But when he picked up the crystal, he realized it was best to keep it all to himself. At least for now, until he could figure out what was going on.

He quickly slipped the first crystal into his trouser's pocket, and the second one into the bag. And he hurried to the office's door. He saw a vertical movement on the door handle, before he even got the time to turn the key gently into the second lock. What could Gustave have been looking for? Perhaps he was looking for the bathroom?

He didn't seem to insist. Albot heard him walk away, and he thought it was a good time to do the same.

While leaving his parents' bedroom, he heard footsteps going up the staircase. He was about to walk back down the hallway, and didn't have time to go back to his room. He felt like a trapped animal. What could he do? He rushed to the bathroom, which was halfway down the corridor, just before Gustav's head appeared at the top of the stairs.

He opened the room's door, and panicked when he saw no one inside. He was about to start calling him when he saw him coming out of the bathroom.

— Where have you been? I didn't hear you walking.

— I went to the bathroom to get my toothbrush and toiletries.

And he showed him the little toilet bag he was holding in his right hand.

— Yes, of course. Excuse me. When I didn't see you in the room anymore, I thought that...

— What did you think? That I sprinted with my crutches, after stepping out of my bedroom window, which is 26 feet high, and jumped ? And then what? What do I do then? Where do I go?

The intonation of his voice betrayed a certain pent-up anger, but Gustave did not notice the tone of his response. He smiled at him, with all his white teeth:

— No, of course not, but I've been asked to keep an eye on you and get you back before nightfall. And the sun's starting to set.

— I'm done, we can go. Could you help me carry my suitcase downstairs, please. I'm not sure I can do it with my crutches.

— Yes, of course. I'll take care of it.

— Wait, I put my laptop underneath my stuff. But I'm afraid I might damage it. I'd like to put it in my backpack, with my game console and my books.

— Wise decision, because the suitcase will travel in the jet's hold, and the jolts may damage it.

— Jet?

— How do you want us to go down South? Moreover, the airfield is closer to our destination than the train station.

He finished packing his suitcase and filled his backpack with the items he wanted to take with him. He stowed the second crystal in the inside left pocket of his jacket without being noticed. And he walked out of the room.

CHAPTER VIII: Hide and seek

When he got to the middle of the stairs, Albot stopped. He thought he saw a shadow moving around in the living room. But he kept walking down, blaming it on his visual fatigue. But they had barely arrived downstairs when a man appeared out of nowhere, pointing a revolver with a silencer at them. No words came out of his mouth, only two muffled noises were heard, as if a bottle of wine was being uncorked.

Gustav immediately collapsed and fell down the last steps of the staircase, finishing his run in the entrance hall. The killer then pointed his gun at Albot. Without saying a word, and before the teenager could say anything, he shot again. The impact of the projectile threw him backwards, and then he blanked…

When he reopened his eyes, he was laying on the floor of the entrance hall, near Gustav, who was laying in a pool of blood. He laid there, on his back, looking up at the ceiling. He needed to come to his senses. He then realized he had been shot. A wave of panic swept him away, and he started looking for his wound, sniffing his clothes for blood. But he didn't find any slimy traces. Was it possible the killer missed him? It was unlikely, there must have been some other explanation.

He ended up noticing a hole in his jacket, where his heart was. He somehow got up, and a bullet fell on the ground. He remembered that he had put the second crystal in the inside pocket of his jacket. The crystal might have been able to dampen the bullet, but how could it have stopped it?

He put his hand inside his pocket, and took out the crystal, which was intact. Not a single scratch! Truly, he was having more and more trouble understanding what was going on around him.

How long had he been unconscious? The room was dark, it was nightfall. He noticed a light at the end of the corridor, coming from his father's study. The killer was still there, apparently looking for something. Could that something be the crystal? One thing he was sure about is that if he didn't find anything, he'd come back to look for it.

He didn't know what to do. Call the police? He hadn't had his cell phone since the accident. He got painfully close to the phone in the hallway, but there was no dial tone, the killer must have made sure to cut the line. He had to search Gustave's body, which was on the ground, for his mobile phone.

He gently approached the driver and started to look in his outside pockets, but didn't find anything. He had to turn him over, in order to search his inside pockets. That wasn't easy to do: Gustav's body was slipping, but he didn't turn around, since he was too heavy. He was about to give up when he heard a muffled noise: it was a phone ringing on vibrate mode, and it seemed to be under the body. He had an idea: he looked for his crutches to use them as a lever. The body moved slightly off the ground, enough to get the mobile phone out of Gustave's jacket, under his blood-stained body.

He managed to drag himself somehow into a cupboard under the stairs, which kind of looked like the one in Harry Potter. He could now answer the call without being noticed. He picked up the phone and a woman's voice could be heard on the other end of the line:

— Hello! Hello! Hello, Gustave. Are you there?

— No, it's not Gustav. It's Albot.

— Albot? Where the hell are you? We agreed that you were supposed to come back before nightfall. And it's almost eight o'clock! Let me talk to Gustave!

— He can't talk to you, he's laying on the floor, at my house, with two bullets in his heart.

— What do you mean? What's going on?

— I don't know, a man showed up at my house and shot us.

— And how are you?

— He also shot me, and apparently he missed his target! But please tell me what to do. Because he's still here, looking through my father's office.

— Try to get out of the house, or hide somewhere he can't find you. I'll call the police and come get you myself.

She hung up. He came out of his hiding place and walked towards the front door. But it was locked. He was trapped. He had to find a place to hide until the police arrived. But he couldn't think of any spot. Then it occurred to him: the stairs from his parents' bedroom to the study... He had to climb the damn stairs again!

He was halfway down the corridor when he heard a noise coming from below. He had to pick up the pace, and he wondered if he had done the right thing by taking his backpack with the computer with him, as the heaviness of the whole thing was making him feel very tired. He heard the killer's footsteps down the hall as soon as he closed his parents' bedroom door. He opened the hidden staircase door and gently closed it behind him. He heard the door on the other side opening with a crash : the killer seemed very angry. He must have been wondering where he went. He heard the bedroom door open a few seconds later, with the same noise. He was right there, so close he could almost hear him breath. What was the police doing?

He sat on the first step, waiting to calm down. He didn't want to move from that place, since that's where he felt safe. But he couldn't stay here forever either, stupidly waiting for the killer to find him, for him to come back, inspect the room and find the entrance to the stairs. He had to get out of there as soon as possible! But how? And where would he go?

Under normal circumstances, he could have gone out through the bedroom window overlooking the garage. But since his physical condition was so bad, he could only imagine the worst-case scenario. But it was either that or a bullet from a revolver...

He slowly came out of his hiding place and tried to listen carefully to the different noises in the house, as the killer must surely have done the same to find him. He went back to close the door of his parents' room, to slow the killer down in case he heard him. He wasn't very reassured to act like an acrobat in his condition.

He was beginning to climb over the bedroom window when the door handle moved, slowly at first, then several times more abruptly. He had to quickly make a decision, otherwise he could either fall from the floor and break his neck or be shot in the head. A cornelian choice between plague and cholera...

The room's door finally opened, after several shots smothered the lock. The door was made of real oak and not cardboard, but the killer must have been in control. When the bedroom door opened, the killer noticed that the window was wide open and that one of the crutches had been left in front of it. He leaned over the window to try to see the teenager on the garage roof, or on the floor. He hesitated about how to proceed, and then took out a device from his pocket to speak to another person.

— Have you seen him?

A voice came out of the device and said:

— What do you mean, did I see him? You lost him?

— How the fuck did you lose a fourteen-year-old cripple who's half blind?

— If we don't settle the score now, we won't get another chance for a while. We need to find him and kill him.

— The others are gonna be pissed...

— I think he jumped through the window and came down through the garage. He can barely walk, so he's probably still close, and in the property.

— Start looking for him, I'll be right down. We've got ten minutes before the cavalry arrives. Then, we'll have to make our way back, before it's too late.

Albot had told himself that there was another way, that he didn't have to choose between plague or cholera. He turned back and hid in the staircase leading down to his father's office. He heard the killer leave the room, and hoped that the cavalry will get there sooner than later, at least before the killers got mad and returned to search the room more carefully.

The ten minutes that passed seemed like an eternity, and the pain medication started to evaporate. Too bad, because, he had twinges in his leg and ribs.

He must have dozed off, because he woke up hearing voices calling for him. He recognized Mrs. Foxter's voice, which reassured him. He slowly opened the door, and found two policemen pointing guns at him. Mrs. Foxter instructed them to lower their guns. He leapt towards her, and then collapsed to the ground, numb with pain from all over his body.

— Please help me get him on the bed until the ambulance arrives.

Two policemen immediately came to help Mrs. Foxter lift Albot off the floor and put him on his parents' bed.

— What the hell happened here? Who are these guys that shot the man downstairs and tried to kill you?

— They are probably thieves, who must have read in the news that the owners had disappeared and wanted to take advantage of an empty home to steal objects, jewelry or money.

— Thieves shooting without any warning? Without asking the slightest question? Pretty strange thieves.

— Thieves who think they are alone, see someone, panic, and start shooting instead of running away.

— There's still something I don't understand: how did they get in and out? This house is under electronic surveillance, the alarm would have gone off.

— They must have disconnected the alarm. They were probably pros.

The first ambulance had arrived. Two paramedics were trying to see if poor Gustave, who was laying on the floor of the entrance hall, was still alive, while a third one went upstairs to see how young Albot was and to check the seriousness of his injuries.

He didn't have any new wounds, he almost had a hole in his heart, but apart from that, he only had the same injuries as those from the accident.

— Okay, we're going to take you to the hospital to check this out, run some tests, make sure you haven't aggravated your previous injuries.

— Mrs. Foxter, could you please keep my backpack and take my suitcase that's already packed?

— Yes, don't worry, I'll take care of everything. I'm going to call in some craftsmen to tidy things up a bit. We had to break down the door to get in. I'm sorry.

— You didn't have much choice, I guess. Call Mrs. Rina, her number is in the phone. She and her husband will tidy things up and she'll clean everything. My parents always said that Mr. and Mrs. Rina were magicians. They will know what they have to do.

The paramedic had injected him with a sedative, to relieve him from the pain and calm him down a little. The effects were starting to kick in. In fact, he couldn't finish his thank you sentence before falling into the arms of Morpheus.

CHAPTER IX: The Attack

He woke up in the hospital again. There was a man standing next to the bedroom door, whom he did not know, but who reacted immediately when he saw that he was awake. He opened the door and spoke to another man who was standing outside.

A few minutes later, Mrs. Foxter came in with a doctor. The doctor examined him, made him do some reflex exercises, which made him feel perplex. Albot felt completely drained, without any physical strength, and his mind was fogged by the medication that was giving to him intravenously. He could no longer remember all the events that had taken place the night before. He was in a semi-comatose state, and was hungry like a wolf.

— So, Doctor, can he be discharged?

— He needs to rest and he won't be able to walk out for a few days. But he's out of danger now, you'll be able to take him home in twenty-four to forty-eight hours.

— No, not tomorrow, and certainly not the day after tomorrow. He has to get out now. He can't stay here, we can't secure the whole hospital. The guards here and the police won't be enough, and I don't want the hospital to witness a shooting.

— I don't understand your ramblings. All I can tell you is that he needs to rest.

— Listen, Doctor. I can't go into details, but the employees and patients of this hospital are in great danger. Believe me, there's nothing that can stop them.

— I don't understand any of your stories, and I don't want to know anything about it. Get him out tonight before the night shift. You'll sign a release of responsibility.

He was walking away when he stopped on the doorstep.

— By the way, I forgot to tell you, there's a certain Detective Colmart who wants to speak with him.

— Tell him he's in no condition to talk right now.

— But he's on his way! He'll be here soon.

— Are you talking about me?

Though Mrs. Foxter was surprised, she didn't act like it.

— Inspector, I was just asking the doctor how we could avoid talking to you.

A smile appeared on the inspector's face, who nevertheless tried to show that he was offended by this comment.

— I can see you're still very straightforward, Helena.

— Mrs. Foxter, Detective Colmart. Please call me Mrs. Foxter.

— My report regarding this attempted murder has already been written and sent to my superiors.

— Does your official report indicate that a thief entered the Coldi home and shot Gustav while young Albot was upstairs? And that he instinctively hid when he heard the sound of the shot?

— I've been used to your little masquerades for a while now, but I would love it if you could answer some of my questions someday, especially regarding certain subjects.

— I don't understand, Inspector. A thief entered the Coldi residence, panicked, fired a gun. That's it! I don't understand your insinuations.

— Mrs. Foxter, either you trust me and I can help you, or you think I'm a fool and I'll leave you to it.

The words « attempted murder » had brought Albot out of his sleepy state. By the time the information was conveyed to the correct neural circuitry, he realized that it implied that Gustav was not dead.

— Excuse me, Mrs. Foxter, but you said « attempted » murder earlier? Is Gustav alive?

— I almost forgot about Gustave. Where is he now, Doctor?

— He's still in the operating room, both bullets hit him in the heart. He should have been killed instantly. But Gustav has a birth defect, and his second heart took over. He lost a lot of blood, but he should be all right.

— Two hearts? Never heard a story like that.

— He is also an orphan. He was abandoned in front of the orphanage when he was born. Probably by parents who couldn't afford his malformation.

— I'm glad he made it through, he's a good guy.

— You'll soon find out he's someone who's way more than that. And I would never have forgiven myself for letting an assassin kill him. Well... I meant a thief, surprised by your arrival.

The inspector noted the information, unnoticed.

— So, what's your plan to get him out of here?

Albot sat on a wheelchair and was carried through the hospital corridors. He was pushed towards an elevator, accompanied by Mrs. Foxter and the two guards posted outside his door. At the same time, another wheelchair, with a child dressed in the same clothes as his, also accompanied by two guards, stopped beside him. He noticed that the jacket he had on wasn't the one he was wearing when he was shot. The child seating next to him had put it on.

— Excuse me, Mrs. Foxter, but I'd like my jacket back.

Mrs. Foxter stared at him:

— What do you mean?

— The boy in that chair has my jacket, and I'd like it back. It's the jacket my parents gave me for my last birthday, and I want it back.

— But it's been damaged, it's got a hole from the bullet.

— I don't care, it's the last thing my parents gave me before they disappeared.

Mrs. Foxter nodded to a guard, indicating him to proceed with the jacket exchange.

A female voice made that recognizable sound, pronouncing the number of the floor, indicating that the elevator doors were going to open on the fifth floor. It showed two men, dressed in turtlenecks and knee-length black coats. Without saying anything, they took out a revolver with a silencer from behind their backs and began to shoot the four guards, who immediately collapsed.

Mrs. Foxter, who was standing right next to Albot, was petrified, and the boy in the wheelchair turned pale. The two killers then directed their weapons at Albot and his doppelgänger. It seemed like they didn't really know how the real Albot Coldi looked like.

— I suggest you give me the crystal immediately, Mrs. Foxter.

Mrs. Foxter understood the request, but didn't act on it.

— What crystal are you talking about?

The only thing that came from one of the killers was the muffled sound of his silencer. Albot turned to the wheelchair next to him, and saw a small hole in the boy's forehead. His eyes, which had remained wide open, expressed his surprise.

— I guess young Coldi won't be able to help us now, I guess, or is Coldi the one who's still alive, standing right in front of us? Either way, Mrs. Foxter, pay attention to what you're going to say.

Mrs. Foxter gave Albot a resigned look, as if she was trying to tell him that they were living their last moments. There heard a bang, that sounded like a big firecracker, but they didn't immediately realize that it couldn't have been from one of the killers' guns because they had silencers.

One of the killers collapsed in the elevator while the second looked around for the source of that mishap. He saw Detective Colmart pointing his service weapon at him as the elevator door closed. The inspector immediately called his colleagues, who were stationed on each of the five floors of the hospital. He ordered them to stand in front of the elevator to arrest the two men. His orders were clear: they could shoot on sight. Without warning.

— Are you two okay?

Mrs. Foxter was speechless and couldn't believe the tragedy she just witnessed. She couldn't utter a single word.

— Yes, we're alright, but call the doctors, so they can see if there's any hope left for them. I don't think you're gonna be able to catch this killer, detective.

— I don't see how he could escape in an elevator. He's not Houdini...

— It's much worse, Detective. You're probably not going to find anything in this elevator. Not a dead person, nor an alive one, no trace of blood, no fingerprints.

A voice, coming from the inspector's walkie-talkie, indicated that his men were inside the elevator, and that there was no one there, dead or alive, which gave credit to what Mrs. Foxter had just said. Not a single drop of blood.

Mrs. Foxter pointed her index finger at the child in the second wheelchair, laying on the ground near the guards. A huge pool of blood was slowly showing underneath him.

— His name is Matthew. Matthew volunteered to help us get you out of here. He was always ready to help others and was a remarkable student. His friends will be devastated to hear about his death. I think the hole in the jacket he was wearing must have made them think it was you! If we had had time to make the exchange, you might have been dead by now.

Mrs. Foxter stooped gently. She closed Matthew's eyes, which had remained open, and carefully removed the jacket before handing it to Albot. When he took the jacket in his hands, he applied slight pressure to the inside pocket without drawing Mrs. Foxter's attention. He wanted to make sure the crystal was still there. It was so light that no one noticed it was even there, but Albot could feel the outline of the object between his fingers.

— I am sad that Matthew died at my feet, because of me. But I'd still like to know why that happened.

The inspector came back with the doctor and some nurses. They were all dismayed by the bodies in front of them. They were used to death, and sometimes even blasé when they saw wounded or dead coming out of the ambulances. But they were surprised by where the crime had been committed. Indeed, it was pretty uncommon to see a killing in a hospital. In the past, an unbalanced person tried to take a doctor hostage because he had committed adultery. But the intervention of the GIGN had quickly put an end to it, via an assault that resulted in the death of the hostage taker and the doctor.

The detective approached Mrs. Foxter and put the gun back in its holster. He had held it in his hand without even realizing it.

— You two! You're gonna have to explain all this shit to me. And keep the unbelievable stories for the orphanage. Because I'm willing to be conciliatory and understanding, but right now, it's gonna be hard to justify five deaths, including one teenager. I hope that your explanations will be more coherent and plausible than those you gave me for the incident at the Coldi residence.

— Detective, we don't have anything specific to explain to you. If you're looking for answers, get close to your superiors so they can, as you said, fill you in. Because I can only give you information that will lead you where you don't want to go.

— You know, I could take you down to the station for questioning?

— You know, by the time I get to the station, our lawyers and your boss will have called you with orders to release us immediately. When we're safe at the Descendance, you'll be able to come and visit us. Maybe that will enlighten you.

The inspector remained dubious for a moment, thinking about what Mrs. Foxter's just said, wondering if she was bluffing.

— I will certainly visit you very soon, as soon as my superiors give me permission to do so.

Mrs. Foxter took out her cell phone, dialed a number and stepped away for a few seconds so that no one could hear what she was saying. Once she was done with her phone call, she turned to the detective.

— You should go home immediately and pack your things.
That's when the inspector's phone rang.

— Good morning Commissioner. Yes sir. Good sir. I understand.

The inspector didn't get a chance to comment on the situation, or give his superior some piece of advice. And when he hung up, his face froze for a few seconds, as if he was trying to process the conversation he just had with his superior.

— Well, Mrs. Foxter, looks like I'll be visiting sooner than expected. I'll be in charge of your security, until you feel like you no longer need me. I've been asked to take another officer with us.

— Well, you've got three hours to make arrangements, we'll leave when you get back.

— I'm going to tell my partner to come with me and then I'll have to go and get some things for the trip. Do I have to pack for a long trip?

— I don't know, but don't bring a lot of things. You'll find everything you need at the Descendance.

— I also have to go down to the police station to fill out certain forms, get some money for expenses and an extra gun or two.

— Do what you have to do, but I want to see you here in three hours. We'll leave immediately after that.

— How are we going to leave?

— Come-back here as scheduled, and I'll explain.

CHAPTER X: The extraction

Detective Colmart had just returned with his right-hand man, Sad Hamler, and was loaded down with two bags and two suitcases.

— You look pretty loaded down, Detective.

— Let's just say I want to be able to deal with any eventuality that might arise during our trip. As a matter of fact, you two should put this on.

The inspector handed them two bulletproof vests.

— What do you want me to do with this, Detective? That wouldn't have protected little Matthew.

— Maybe, but they don't always aim for the head.

— You're right, Detective, but I'm not putting that thing on.

— Either you put it on voluntarily, or I'll need to force you to put it on. It's up to you.

— We're already equipped, Detective, don't worry about us. We've taken advantage of these few hours to do so.

— What do you mean, you're equipped?!

— By the way, get your vest off me, Detective, and put this on.

Mrs. Foxter took out two boxes that looked quite light, which she handed to the inspector and his assistant. The boxes contained a sort of long-sleeved black t-shirt and a type of tights that looked like those you would wear to go skying.

— They're one size fits all. You will find on the label on the collar a sort of dot. When you'll squeeze it, the clothes will adapt to your morphology. These garments are « breathable », like a sports garment, and balance the body's temperature. But they are also able to stop high impact and close range shots. We've just received them.

— Where do they come from?

— More like when did they came in, Detective. More like when did they came in... but it's a long story, and we don't have time for explanations.

Just know that I needed to get a lot of permits to give you this material. Once you press the dot, this garment will belong to you for life, and no one else will be able to use it but you, or else you they will die from suffocation.

— I don't even understand what you're saying, and now you're talking about things that only exist in science fiction movies.

— I'm just asking you to trust me, Inspector, and if you have any questions, you can ask them when we get back down to the Descendance.

— So I'm just gonna put this thing on, and I'll call you if I choke...

— Leave your finger on the label for a few seconds so that the garment can record the information.

The inspector was about to bounce back on this last remark when he recalled that his supervisor had received instructions directly from the Minister, and that he was told to make himself available to Mrs. Foxter without question.

— All right, ma'am, we'll put this shirt and these tights on, without asking any questions, and we'll talk when we're safe. So, what's your plan to get us out of here? And when do we leave?

— There is a van waiting for us in the basement of the hospital, a taxi at the entrance, a laundry truck behind the hospital and a helicopter on the terrace.

— That gives us a lot of possibilities, but it doesn't give me the option that you've chosen?

— What about you, Detective, what would you choose?

— Apart from being a soothsayer or making an educated guess on each option, I don't see how you would know what we would have chosen in advance, since we haven't even made our decision yet.

— I'm going to ask you, Inspector, to find a way to shut down all the surveillance cameras in the hospital, then shut down the telephone and Internet circuits in the facility for about 15 minutes, and finally unlock and unblock all the alarms on the hospital's access doors. I want this hospital to go deaf and mute for about 15 minutes.

— I'll see what I can do, but it may take a while.

— You have half an hour to figure it out, then we'll have to leave.

The inspector returned thirty-five minutes later. He seemed out of breath, but his cheerful face indicated that he must have managed to find a solution.

— In five minutes, this entire neighborhood, including the hospital, will suffer from a general power outage. The generators will take over in less than ten seconds. This switchover from the generator will keep the minimum subsistence in service in order to preserve maximum energy. This is about the amount of time you needed, with an added bonus of switching off the outside lights.

— Good idea, Detective.

The inspector looked at his watch and called someone on the phone. A few seconds later, the hospital corridors were plunged into darkness. With the immediate switch to emergency mode, the dimmer light indicated that the generator had taken over. Lights in the stairwells were also dimmed, with the new low-power LED technology taking over in the event of a power outage. The lighting was less consistent, but still provided good visibility.

Inspector Colmart led the way, followed by Mrs. Foxter who was pushing young Coldi's wheelchair and Sad, the inspector's partner, who brought up the rear. The handsome young man walked straight down the fire stairs and began to descend without meeting anyone. They had folded the wheelchair, and the inspector was carrying young Coldi, who could barely stand.

Downstairs, Mrs. Foxter took a break. She took out her phone, which was still working despite the power outage in the neighborhood: the telephone antennas of the various telecommunications providers had an inverter that could last a few hours. She only said one thing:

— Go!

A few seconds passed before they heard a muffled sound coming from the roof, followed by several explosions.

— Ouch, apparently our friends don't want to take any chances and have chosen to destroy all of our options.

« Go » was the signal for all options to leave the hospital at the same time. Luckily there was no one in the different vehicles, as they were all remotely controlled.

— What do we do now?

— We're still going down. We still have some time, before our little friends realize what they've done.

They continued their descent, crossing several corridors of pipes, the ones that bring power and communications to the hospital.

— But where are we going, Mrs. Foxter?

— We just got out of the hospital, Detective.

They arrived in front of a first security door. Mrs. Foxter took out a magnetic card : she presented it to the door, which emitted a small beep, validating and triggering its opening on a vast room where various devices and materials were piled up, wrapped in bubble wrap or white cloth to protect them from dust.

— What is this place?

— This is the hospital's old bomb shelter, which has become a storage room over time or, occasionally, a warehouse.

— But what are we doing here?

— Nothing, we keep going and we hurry to enter this room and close this door, because in thirty seconds, the power will be back on and the camera that records this corridor will work again and film us.

So they hurried in and closed the door behind them. They say that the lights in the corridor came back as soon as they shut the door.

— I hope the guys upstairs at the security desk didn't see the door close!

— What is this place?

— As I have already told you, it is an old bomb shelter from World War II, which has since been converted into a storage room, as you can see.

— This room you call anti-atomic seems strange to me!

— Let's just say it is what it seems to be without being what it is. But the most important thing is that it's our way out.

Mrs. Foxter looked at the room, spinning around for a few seconds, before declaring:

— Mr. Hamler, could you please push that cart in the left corner?

Mr. Hamler executed himself, but nothing in particular appeared on the floor, not the slightest sign of opening. Mr. Hamler's face showed a certain perplexity. Mrs. Foxter came closer, bent down and again presented her badge to the floor. A beep was heard, indicating that it had recognized the card.

— But how did you know you had to show your badge here?

A hatch in the opposite corner lifted up thanks to a jack mechanism — it must have weighted a lot — revealing ladder steps that allowed people to get in or out of the room.

— You just have to find what you're looking for, and that will tell you what the right place is.

— I don't understand what you just said.

— Look at the ceiling and not the floor.

— I don't see anything special, it's rough concrete.

— Stand in the center of the room and look at the ceiling again.

Mr. Hamler executed himself: he looked carefully at the ceiling and couldn't see anything.

— I still don't see anything special.

— Nothing in particular is nothing. And what's nothing special?

— Just some porosity on the ceiling, I guess, due to the rough concrete, and I can see small holes in certain areas.

— Now, take my glasses and look again.

Mr. Hamler was surprised by the fact that most of the holes were no longer visible. Now, he could only see some of them.

— I see clusters of holes in several places.

— And now close your left eye.

Mr. Hamler was surprised and kept his mouth wide open without being able to make a sound.

— Judging by your blissful face, I guess you understand now.

— Now, I see, but I'm not sure I understand.

— Just know that if you misinterpret the sign among all those you can see, and present the key in the wrong place, you may quickly find yourself burned to death. I will not give you any further explanation. That way, you won't be able to talk about things you didn't know if you're questioned.

This last sentence left everyone skeptical and casted a chill.

— I guess we have to go downstairs?

— Yes, and watch out for young Coldi, because he can barely stand. Hold him to help him down.

There were about fifteen steps to go, which was not a major problem for the small group, who soon found itself on firm ground. It was pretty dark, but they could still see a bit thanks to the light coming out of the hatch opening. Mrs. Foxter held her badge in front of the opening, which again made a small sound that indicated that the system recognized the magnetic card, causing the hatch to close and leaving them in a stressful darkness.

— Which way are we going?

— Let's wait a few seconds for the light to come back.

After a minute or two, a light slightly illuminated the place, but it was impossible to determine the origin of the light source. Their eyes had to get used to the dim light so that they could see through the tunnels.

— I hope you have a map of these galleries, Mrs. Foxter... Because I don't know how we are going to know which way is the right way.

— Because you're looking in the wrong place again and with the wrong eyes.

She walked to the three galleries and inspected them one by one. She then took her phone out, tapped the screen, directed it to the ground and then to the top of each tunnel's entrance. She finally said:

— Let's take the one on the left.

— Why this one and not one of the others?

— Because it's written.

They looked at each other without saying anything. Sad unfolded the wheelchair and the inspector put young Coldi back on it.

— What are we waiting for? Let's go !

They walked for about half a kilometer in the dark, while the temperature in the tunnel kept going down.

— Why is it so cold, Mrs. Foxter?

Mrs. Foxter took some gloves out of her backpack and handed them out.

— I didn't give them to you at the same time as the first equipment, because I didn't want to waste any time explaining why you would need to wear gloves during that time of the year. As soon as you will put them on, the gloves will automatically be calibrated with the rest of your equipment, so don't panic if your fingertips tingle a bit. Also, put these kind of socks on. The material needs some time to adjust. But don't take them off, under any circumstances, for the next two hours. Otherwise the synchronization between everything will be corrupted and the garments will lose their properties. One last thing : we're going to experience intense cold, followed by equally intense heat. I'm also going to give you hoods with no holes in them. Once again, don't panic, this material allows oxygen and light to pass through. But it also needs about an hour to adjust to your environment and your morphology. So we will be in complete darkness for an hour, including myself, because, as I have already explained, this material is also new to me.

    — Yet you seem to have it under control.

    — It was presented to me a while ago, but it was still being developed.

    — Do you work for the army or special services, ma'am?

Mrs. Foxter smiled.

    — No, I don't work for anyone. But let's say that the government has common interests with us, which allows us to find certain compromises and establish some mutual assistance. Now, put this on, and let's sit down on the floor for a couple of hours. I hope no-one's claustrophobic? Oh, and wait! I forgot the most important thing. You have to trust me: here is a pill that you need to swallow.

    — I don't swallow anything without a doctor's prescription, and especially without knowing what it is.

    — Well, if you refuse to take this pill, you won't be able to follow us and you'll be forced to stay here and wait for our friends.

    — Don't be stupid, Sad. Just swallow this shit and get it over with.

    — But this is just the beginning, Detective, not the end.

The inspector's puzzled look showed that he didn't fully comprehend what was going on. He was completely overwhelmed.

Everyone swallowed their capsule and sat on the ground for two hours. Being inactive in this temperature should have froze them, but once they had the clothes on, they did not feel any discomfort from the low temperature.

— With the equipment you are wearing, your body temperature will be regulated. The outside temperature could still decrease or increase without you feeling the slightest difference.

— Indeed, I can only feel the cold on my feet and fingers.

— Yes, it takes some time to adjust. Soon, you won't feel the difference. Stop talking now, and try to get some sleep.

— But what was in those pills?

— Just *nanotriaminums*. I'll explain later.

CHAPTER XI: The hunt

Electricity had returned to the hospital area. Everything was back to normal, but the same could not be said regarding the staff. The destruction of the helicopter on the roof, the taxi in front of the entrance and the laundry van in the back of the hospital had made the staff panic, as well as the patients.

Firefighters and the police were all focused on the destruction, trying to put out the fires and transport the injured. Journalists and onlookers were kept away by several policemen who tried to keep them at a safe distance thanks to a security perimeter. A crisis cell was immediately opened within the main departments involved, in order to coordinate all actions and decisions. It was absolute chaos. The flames from the various fires that had broken out during the night created thick smoke. The flashing lights of the various units working on the site gave the impression of war. And chaos often makes things that are usually out of the ordinary invisible.

The elevator beeped, followed by the number of the floor, indicating that it had arrived at its destination. The doors opened and two men appeared. One of these two men was already there a few hours earlier.

— The security station is located right behind the elevators that lead to the main entrance.

— What do we do, master?

— We ask them to show us the last two hours of footage from the surveillance cameras.

— What if they refuse, master?

The master did not answer his young assistant's question. But he also realized that they had already drawn quite a lot of attention to themselves with all the shootings and explosions. He had to try to re-establish dialogue with people, despite the orders he had received. He had been given free rein to carry out this mission, but he did not understand why he had to eliminate the young boy named Coldi. However, he was not asked to understand the motives, just to carry out the orders.

They approached the security station. They tried to get in, but the door was locked. There was an intercom with a camera at the entrance. The master pressed the intercom button, and an answer was immediately heard over the loudspeaker:

— Hello, how can I help you?

They looked at each other, not knowing what to say.

— We're from the police, and we're here to look at some footage, to try to figure out what the hell's going on out here.

— Hold on, we're going to let you in.

After a few seconds, a beep, followed by the sound of the electric strike controlling the lock, invited them in. They entered and saw that there were two guards, that were carrying weapons, inside the room.

— What can we do for you, gentlemen?

— As I just told you, we would like to see the last two hours of footage.

— Precisely, we were in the process of stalling the video server. We wanted to go back over the attack this afternoon near the elevators.

— We just want to watch the last two hours.

— Didn't Detective Colmart send you?

The master and his assistant looked at each other and pulled out their weapons.

— Gentlemen, I asked you something specific, so let's stop arguing, I don't have time.

— What the hell is the matter with you?

At the same time, the video of the first attack, that occurred during the afternoon, appeared on the screen. One of the two men who was in front of the guards could be seen in the video. The two guards looked at each other, and froze. One of the guards tried to get up, but a searing pain went through his chest. He stopped moving, then looked down at the spot where the pain came from and saw a red mark that began to spread over his white shirt. He had a last thought for his daughter Milena, which brought tears to his eyes. His wife had disappeared a few months earlier, killed by cancer, which made him a widower and left his daughter without a mother. And he collapsed...

— But why did you shoot him? We're not even armed. It was a reflex to stand up, not an attack!

The master was tired of all this killing, and was starting to like the situation less and less. The young accomplice, who had remained calm, was pointing his weapon at the second guard when the master intervened:

— No, wait, we don't have much time.

— Can you show us the last two hours of the surveillance cameras?

The guard, who was on his knees next to his colleague, trying to stop the bleeding, did not answer but asked for help:

— Somebody call 911, please!

The shooter remained impassive.

— We're in a hurry. We don't have time to lose.

The guard got up, nodded and looked at his young colleague laying at his feet, where a small pool of blood was beginning to appear. The guard moved closer to the console and entered some commands on the computer.

With his mouse, he started validating things by clicking on some icons on the screen.

— It's going to take a few minutes, because, thanks to the power outage, the cameras have been shut down.

— We want to watch the ten minutes preceding the outage and the ten minutes that followed.

The guard looked at his watch, and typed in the time he was supposed to look for into the computer.

— What exactly would you like to see?

— Just show me the different cameras, I'll tell you what to do.

— Is it possible to show all recordings simultaneously?

— In theory, yes, but our server has not been calibrated for this kind of search, the processor is not powerful enough.

The master nodded and looked at his partner.

— Where is that server?

— It's in the back room.

— My partner will take care of this power processor problem.

The partner went to the room and returned a few moments later.

— You can start looking at all the footage on all the screens now.

The guard went on wondering how processing an image could be increased five times in such a short period of time. He launched a new command on the console, convinced that an error message would appear indicating that his request could not be taken into account. But instead, all the screens lit up and showed the recorded images. Scrolling through the images at high speed on so many screens could have made anyone dizzy.

— Stop! Where is this camera located?

— It faces the elevators on the fifth floor.

You could see four people chatting. The screen went black right after one of them looked at his watch.

— How long did the blackout last?

— About 15 minutes.

— Let's move forward to when the power returned.

That's what the guard did. The images reappeared.

— Stop! Where's that camera?

— It's in a basement, I don't know where exactly. But there's nothing there. Just a hallway leading to a door.

— Rewind on that camera, and play it back in slow motion.

— I don't see anything, master.

— Stop!

You could see a slight door movement. It was imperceptible to the eye of a normally constituted human being.

— Where is that camera?

— I don't know! Normally, I don't even put it in view mode, because there's never anything there.

— What does the coding that appears on the screen indicate? BCCL7?

— Basement camera corridor level 7, but it doesn't show the exact location. It could be anywhere.

— If something goes wrong, how do you find your way around it?

— We have a manual.

— Show it to me.

The guard stood up, trying not to walk into the pool of pool his colleague was laying in. He had the most serious doubts about his chances of making it out alive. But what could he do? He would have tried to push the panic button, but that speakers would have asked him what the problem was. The only chance he had of getting out of this mess was if a real policeman came along. He could pray, but he wasn't a fervent Catholic, and was afraid that his prayer wouldn't be heard.

He opened the binder where the camera shots were arranged. He had one last doubt and wondered if he should try to negotiate his life.

— So? Are you finding anything?

— Yes, I got it. There you go.

They flipped through the table of contents and went to the chapter that indicated « video camera positioning ». After going through the type of camera, the reference number, wiring diagram and parameterization, they got to the « positioning » chapter. They looked for the camera coding.

— The map only shows the physical location, not how to get there, master.

— It's not Google Maps, replied the guard. You'd have to have access to their online maintenance tools to get such detailed information.

— What do you mean? Explain what you mean by that.

The guard looked at the clock hanging on the wall and wondered whether it would be better to tell them everything so they would leave quickly, or to wait for the day shift to arrive, which would be there in about 30 minutes, hoping they would get here earlier. But what would happen if the team showed up? These two crazy men would not hesitate one second, and shoot them.

— So?

— Yes, sorry. I was just thinking. We should have access to the maintenance tool of the company in charge of managing the site. But I don't have the password to access it. And if you get it wrong three times, it blocks the system, and there won't be any way to access it.

— Show me the home page.

The security guard executed himself. The master looked at his partner and nodded, to confirm his order. The young guard placed an object he had taken out of his pocket on the computer. The system beeped a little, and several jerky images appeared on the control screen before the home page appeared, as well as the search engine.

— Here you go, master. We can start the research.

After a few minutes of consultation, they found what they were looking for: they had located the camera.

— What do we do now, master?

— Take the modules back to the server and the computer, erase everything and wait for me in front of the elevators, I'll be there in a few seconds.

The young partner left the room without worrying about the guard. The master turned around and walked towards the guard, taking out his weapon and pointing it at him.

— I'm going to shoot you. Don't move if you want to live.

The guard didn't understand what the killer meant, but he felt a searing pain in his heart. The bullet almost touched his heart, but didn't cause too much damage, which would allow him to be saved if someone quickly came to help him. The master turned away, leaving the guard slumped on his seat with a stunned look on his face.

— If I were you, I'd call 911, because you're losing a lot of blood, and in about a minute, you're going to pass out.

The master joined his partner, who was waiting for him in front of the elevators. There was not the slightest sign of compassion on his face.

— What do we do, master? Do we look for them and eliminate them?

The master wasn't sure what to say. He didn't want to answer, but he had to, because his apprentice wouldn't hesitate for a second to eliminate him if he had the slightest doubt about him.

And on top of that, he'd be rewarded for reacting to an imposter. So he was forced to answer:

— We find them, and we take them all out after we take the crystal.

Half an hour latter, the two killers arrived at the armored door, which could only be open with a badge. Once again, they took the same object out of their pockets and presented it to the badge reader. The LEDs flashed alternately, turning red and green for a few seconds, before a beep was heard, followed by the sound of the various jacks releasing the door.

— I don't think their surveillance system will be working again anytime soon, master!

— I'd rather be suspicious towards these people. They are so strange, I can't understand their emotions and their limits. As much as we know what we are destined to do in our society, I have the impression that this society is archaic and without any ambition.

— I don't understand them either! They're like insects that we could easily crush, why should we go through so much trouble with them? But my greatest astonishment comes from their physical resemblance to us and their multiple languages. I wonder what's the point of having so many different languages? It's a good thing we have our own *Symlium*, that allows us to communicate with them, because I could hardly imagine having to learn their dialects.

— Let's go in now and see where they are.

They entered the room, which seemed empty.

— Close the door, so we won't be disturbed.

— Where did they go, master?

CHAPTER XII: The Tunnel

The small group had slightly fallen asleep for two hours. They woke up trying to remember where they were.

— I think we can go back now.

— Did the synchronization went well, Mrs. Foxter? We look like Fantomas with our masks.

— Yes, Albot, we can make sure it did by looking at the chrominance that comes out of the clothes: they have slightly changed color and are visible to the naked eye. The synchronisation of signals between the different elements result in a kind of molecular adhesion with the *nanodes*.

— *Nanodes?* I thought you only mastered the technology in the lab?

— Let's just say our friends are a little ahead of the game. Let's take advantage of what we're offered and save the questions for later.

— But how do they charge?

— They work like power plants. They charge thanks to your body temperature, when it hits thirty-six degrees Celsius.

Mrs. Foxter took four objects, that looked like watches but were as flat as three sheets of paper put together, out of her bag:

— Wrap this around your left wrist.

— A watch?

— Indeed, it also gives the time and date, but if you press the two top buttons, it will give you all the information about yourself: heartbeat, body temperature and outside temperature, calories expended, humidity level, etc.. I will give you a small practical guide when we arrive at the Descendance. For now, just remember one important piece of information: the dial can turn into four different colors. As long as your dial is blue, everything is fine. But if it turns orange, there's something wrong. The unit can self-diagnose and repair itself, but you will have to stand still again.

— What about the other two colors?

— I'm getting there. Problems rarely happen, but there is no such thing as zero risk. If it turns red, I advise you to remove the suit as soon as possible.

— Why would we do that?

— Let's just say that you could find yourself in a tight, cramped space. The color white will tell you that the suit is in self-healing mode. For the moment, only remember that the other features will be communicated to you later or during our little trip. And for Fantomas, you're right, Albot. Press the button on the bottom left of the device on your wrist.

The masks began to become transparent, until everyone's face appeared.

— What do we do now?

— We're going to take this tunnel, and don't dawdle, we're going to walk straight through it without stopping.

— Where does that tunnel lead us?

— Somewhere where we'll be safe. At least, I hope so... And I almost forgot: this is a bag that has the same properties as your suits. You have to put everything you have in it: coins, watch, belt buckle, bracelet, gun, etc...

— It's like we're in an airport. What about the wheelchair? What do we do about the wheelchair?

— We'll leave it here, but we'll have to share the burden. Inspector, you'll have to carry young Coldi, do you feel like you can do that?

— How much do you weigh, Albot?

— About 77 pounds, sir. Why?

— It should be all right, but I have a feeling it's going to be a long ride.

— You, Mr. Hamler, will carry the bag.

— Why do we need to take all these precautions?

— As I explained, but perhaps not clearly enough, the cold and hot zones we're about to pass through will damage these objects. It may injure you, or even kill you.

— When you say hot and cold zones, what kind of temperatures are we talking about?

— Let's say they're close to cryogenic temperature and close to the lava temperature of a volcano.

— You want me to believe that this tunnel is made up of the lowest temperature that can exist, which is about -240 degrees, in Fahrenheit, and that it can also be close to the temperature of the lava, which varies between 1300 and 2200 degrees, in Fahrenheit?

— Yes, and with an electromagnetic energy level close to a thousand teslas.

— And you want to get us in there, in those pajamas you gave us?

— Look, there's no other way. Either we go through it, or we stay and go back, but I think our friends are following us and they'll catch up with us soon. These suits are designed for these environments and can withstand all this. But we wouldn't be able to stop, because they can't work forever. Once we enter the first zone, we won't be able to stop. There is no emergency stop button. If one of us were to stop, we would not be able to start again. This tunnel is a thousand meters long. But I want you to know that you'll have to walk those 3280 feet as fast as you can, without stopping.

— I don't understand anything you're saying.

— Look, do as you please. I'm going, gentlemen, and I'll carry young Coldi if I have to.

There was a moment of silence, during which the inspector wondered what he had gotten himself into.

— What are we waiting for? Come on, let's go!

The small group arrived in front of the place where the tunnel was supposed to start, as there was no indication whatsoever. The inspector signaled to the young Coldi to get on his back. He took a deep breath, as if he were to snorkel in the sea, and went forward. He had already walked 1000 feet with young Coldi on his back, and he wondered if he would make it to the end. He didn't feel the cold, but his clothes were brittle, his jacket was in shreds because of the friction of young Coldi's body. All of his clothes had turned white because of the intense cold in the tunnel. He was bringing up the rear with more and more questions about the Descendance.

— Helena, I can't do it. I can't stand it anymore.

— We're almost halfway there, Detective. We've still got about 2000 feet to go.

— Is that supposed to make me feel better?

— When you can no longer do this, press all three buttons on your device at the same time. But only do it in case of an emergency. The nanodes will be able to help you, but for no longer than five minutes. After that, they will go into standby mode and you won't have any protection anymore.

They had passed the cold zone and were halfway through the hot zone. They had about 800 feet to go when the inspector collapsed with young Coldi.

— Come on! On your feet, Detective, we're almost there.

Mrs. Foxter approached the inspector and pressed the three keys on the dial. The nanodes went into emergency mode, amplifying every muscle in their host.

— Mr. Hamler, I advise you to do the same on your device, because we can't stop. Now, we only have one minute left to get out of here.

The inspector felt his strength increase drastically. He stood up again, with young Coldi in his arms, and began to sprint, followed by his colleague and Mrs. Foxter. The dial of the device began to change color and turned orange : they started feeling the warmth of the environment on their skin. They tried to run faster. The inspector closed his eyes like a sprinter trying to cross the Olympic finish line, except that there was no landmark to help him find his way and he collapsed.

When he came back to his senses, he was surrounded by young Coldi, Hamler and Mrs. Foxter.

— So, Detective, did you want to train for the next Olympics?

His mouth was parched. He felt paralyzed and exhausted.

— Don't worry, the nanodes are in standby and self-repair mode, so don't move.

— Yes, but who's gonna fix my shoes? The cold and then the heat got the best of my old Westons. When I think about how much I paid for them, and the love I gave them to make them look brand new.

— I see you've kept your sense of humor, Detective. We'll buy a new pair when we get out of this mess. From now on, we can take our time. I don't think our friends are equipped for this kind of expedition.

— What if they are?

— Maybe they're wearing pajamas too. But I don't think their module is compatible.

— What do you mean?

— The enormous magnetic field in this tunnel are also useful to our nanodes because it helps them withstand the overload of these extreme temperatures. Our nanodes are fed with our body's temperature, and that's how they function, as I told you. But they also use the Earth's magnetic field and radio waves to power themselves when needed. And in this case, the magnetic field is encoded to work only with your modules. Otherwise, the nanodes would be inhibited halfway through, and you probably figured out what would happen if that was the case...

— Of course, I wouldn't like to be out of order halfway through. I can't even imagine what would happen.

— At minus 258 degrees, in Fahrenheit, you are instantly frozen and at 1832 degrees, you literally melt. In both cases, you have no time to suffer, your death is instantaneous.

— One question comes to my mind: how did we manage to breathe in these extreme temperatures?

— And to run? added the inspector.

— *Nanodes* are capable of turning water into oxygen, and your sweat is mostly water. In this case, they convert your sweat into oxygen to help you breathe. Nanodes behave like a second skin, they will soon even be able to repair human tissue, after a burn or a small wound. They can update their codes just like a computer, but they can also communicate with each other. Let me show you how.

Mrs. Foxter grabbed the inspector's hand and his module immediately turned the same color as the inspector's.

— My module is making contact with yours to see how my nanodes can help.

Both the inspector's and Mrs. Foxter's modules turned a bluish tint indicating that the self-repair was complete.

— Our systems have combined to speed up the repair process.

— So what do we do now?

— We're almost there and we'll be able to rest while we get our strength back.

— Yes, but where are we exactly?

— In a place that's a little further away than where we were before.

— A little further? Could you be a little more specific ? I'm a little suspicious since you told us about the temperatures in the tunnel.

— We're under the tundra. There you go.

— Is that a neighborhood Paris?

— No, Mr. Hamler, it's...

— Don't tell me you're talking about the tundra in Antarctica?

— We are under a dormant volcano, about ten minutes away from our destination.

— Except I don't understand how on earth we ended up here! And what the hell are we doing here anyway?

— We can talk about it when we get to the site. Now, get up and let's move.

The inspector rolled his eyes to show them that they were delirious. But he was too tired to make any complaints, and he felt too disoriented by all the information he had to absorb and understand. All he wanted right now was a shower and a nice bed. But he wasn't convinced that the destination they were heading to was going to give them what he was waiting for.

They had been walking up the mountain for ten minutes. The interior lighting was produced by a sort of paint and emanated from the floor and the walls. This made it possible to move around, without replacing the light from the lamps. They arrived in front of a rocky wall. Mrs. Foxter took something out of her pocket and placed it in a gap. A small noise was heard, which echoed through the cave where they were standing. But nothing happened. She tried again, twice, but nothing more than a beep happened.

— What's going on, Mrs. Foxter?

— The system refuses to recognize my key!

— And what do we do now? Can we get out of here?

— The only passage is this one, or the tunnel where we came from. And our suits won't be able to withstand another passage this close in the tunnel.

— So what do we do now?

— Honestly, I don't know... We're a little, how can I say that... stuck.

The sentence cast a chill over the small group. They could neither move forward nor backward, and they were starting to feel hungry.

— When you say key, what do you mean? Cause I don't see any locks on this damn door.

— I use the term key, but it is not literally a key, as you can imagine. It's a kind of crystal that has a certain property, one of which is that it can emit a code by resonance on a certain wavelength to unlock certain doors. But apparently, not this one...

— Isn't there any other way to open this fucking door?

— If any of you have one of these crystals, now is the time to say so.

She was kind of joking, and never would have had imagined that it would resonate with Albot.

— Actually, ma'am, I may have another crystal. I don't know if it'll help us open this door, but we can always try.

All eyes turned to Albot, and he had the strange feeling that he was in the shoes of a petty thief who had just been caught.

— What do you mean you have a crystal? Where'd you get it? Who gave it to you?

Albot was completely confused by all these questions, and he was not willing to provide any information on the subject until he knew who he was dealing with.

— My father gave it to me, he lied.

— What's your father got to do with this?

— It's a long story, Mr. Sad. And this is neither the time nor the place to debate about it. We'll deal with it later.

— Give me your crystal so I can try it on this door!

Albot put his hand in the inside pocket of his coat, but an unpleasant sensation made him panic.

— My crystal's gone! Shit, where is it? I'm sure I had it in my pocket before I went into the damn tunnel. I'm sure because I checked while we were sitting around, waiting for our suits to sync up. I can only think of one explanation : it must have fallen out when the inspector collapsed on me. The coat must have been badly damaged by the cold, and the pocket must have broke. I've got to go back in there and get it.

— You're in no condition to do so, Albot. The inspector is shattered, and Mrs. Foxter's suit is still in self-diagnosis mode. I'm the only one who can do it.

— Mr. Hamler is unfortunately right. He is the only one who can go back immediately. Mr. Hamler, come closer so I can check your control module. Um, you just have enough power to get there and come back without loitering.

— What does this crystal look like?

Mrs. Foxter took hers out of her pocket and handed it to the deputy inspector. He was surprised by its lightness.

— That's your crystal thing? Looks like a simple piece of glass. I mean, for all I know about technology... I just got rid of my old Minitel... So if you tell me it's a key, then we'll call it a key. As long as that thing gets us out of here.

Mrs. Foxter looked up but made no comment.

— Look, Mr. Hamler, you only have about seven minutes to go there and come back. I'm going to program your module to ring halfway through and one minute before time runs out. Your suit's in no condition to go into Superman mode, so you're on your own. Save yourself, save your strength for the return trip, don't run on the outward journey. I'll accompany you to the tunnel entrance.

— No, *we'll* go with you.

She turned to Albot, and was about to open her mouth to say no. But she decided not to say anything when she saw in the child's eyes his willingness to go with him. As for the inspector, he was sound asleep.

— Let's not waste any time. Let's go. Let the inspector rest, he's in no condition to come with us.

And the small group walked towards the entrance of the tunnel.

— Mr. Hamler.

— Call me Sad, please.

— Sad, above all, be careful, don't take any unnecessary risks.

— By the way, what do I do if I come face to face with our pursuers?

The question remained unanswered. Sad had already started to walk away, without waiting.

CHAPTER XIII: The rescue

The master had managed to decode the room's opening system, and had used the same trap door. He and his partner had managed to find the right gallery, thanks to the footprints on the floor, and they had almost arrived in front of the tunnel. The master stopped. He had sensed that something was wrong. He had noticed traces on the ground, as if the group they were tracking had stopped there for a while. He wondered why they would have done such a thing, when they knew they were being chased by killers.

— What's going on, master?

— Haven't you noticed the cold is getting worse?

— Yes, but I mostly feel it on my face, because my suit protects me from everything else.

— Something's wrong. This isn't right. Let's put our masks and gloves on. Because, from what I can remember, this tunnel looks like one of the first passages that were ever built here.

— I don't understand, master.

At the time, the Europeans had built a particle accelerator with a diameter of twenty-seven kilometers, and researchers had placed great hope in this instrument. What they wanted to find during their research was the Higgs boson, which they considered to be the holy grail of research. They tried to delay the start of this one with a few interventions to discourage them, without trying to bring too much attention to themselves. We had already intervened in the past in the United States on one of their accelerators, and it was difficult to do the same with this one.

— And then what happened next?

— What was bound to happen happened... They created some kind of black hole, which is like opening Pandora's box. In the beginning, all the scientists celebrated this discovery, all the heads of state of the world wanted to come and see, as in a museum, the phenomenon. But, during one of these visits, an incident occurred, killing one head of state and his entire staff. The black hole had doubled in size and the people around it were sucked in. They made it look like a plane crash, they recovered the bodies of strangers, burned them and sent them back home, and no one really said anything about it. The problem is that once the black hole was created, they did not have the competence to control it. It was an accidental discovery, for which they were not prepared. The hole was unstable and growing at a rapid rate, threatening to destroy everything. The scientific community took turns for months without success. That's when our organization came together to determine whether we should intervene, help or not. After several rather virulent debates, there was a split. A majority decided to do nothing, while a minority wanted to intervene. The minority created its own organization and decided to secretly send a representative to help them close this black hole. A scientist volunteered to go there with no possibility of return, because the minority did not have the infrastructure to return.

— That scientist's name was Hernest Ziegler. He had the skills to control this black hole but did not know how to approach governments and scientists to convince them of his good faith. He was afraid they would think he was crazy, and that they would put him in a psychiatric ward or a prison. He decided to send documents containing unknown mathematical formulas to the world's leading researchers of the time to get their attention, and then he introduced himself to them.

— Scientists were skeptical at first. But after he explained the solution, the most industrialized governments and their most recalcitrant researchers gathered behind closed doors to listen to him. It took them almost two years to control the black hole and transform it into a core with a high energy potential that was no longer a danger to humanity. Ziegler had incorporated a mathematical formula into the transformation of the nucleus, hoping he could find a way home. But on our side, we were able to introduce one of our agents into the scientific conglomerate, who managed to tamper with the formulas, creating a time tunnel to eliminate Ziegler.

— All the countries wanted to participate in this adventure because they already saw all the benefits they could gain from it in terms of technological progress. They built a tunnel powered by this core below the particle accelerator, saying that the work that had been done was just an addition and a modification of the particle accelerator. Once the tunnel was completed, people started talking about temperature stability problems, but I'm not sure what it was all about. They first shipped robots, but the extreme temperature was not conducive to this technology. Then, they sent soldiers and scientists in special suits. But they never came back. The craze was short. A global financial crisis we organized made it difficult to continue the research because of a lack of budget. And everyone went home with their tails between their legs. The tunnel remained as it was...

— You mean it's still working?

— I think so. And we're going to find out very quickly. I don't know where it will lead us, though.

When they entered the first zone, they could see on the controllers' dials that they were wearing on their wrists the dizzying drop in temperature, that lowered to minus 1850 degrees, in Fahrenheit.

— It's a good thing, master, that you reacted, we would have died instantly. We wouldn't even had time to realize what was happening...

— No, indeed.

The master was scrolling on his dial, looking at the information about his suit. When he reached the electromagnetic parameter, he froze.

— Quick, throw your gun down and any metal objects you have in your pockets.

They barely had time to get rid of their weapons, which had turned white due to the extreme temperature in the tunnel. The weapons broke into dozens of pieces as soon as they hit the ground. Even the bullets shattered, letting the powder and the balls spill out onto the ground.

— And the other weapons, master?

— The alloy they're made out of, which is titanium and carbon, protects them from this kind of disadvantage. Let's keep going.

— Master, look over there! It seems like someone's coming...

— You're right.

Sad was approaching the spot where the inspector had fallen with young Coldi, but he couldn't see anything on the ground and began to feel desperate. His module indicated that he had less than thirty seconds to find the object before he had to go back. He refused to imagine coming back empty-handed. Because even though he wasn't sure if the damn crystal would open the damn door, he was still their only hope. Sad was too preoccupied looking down on the ground for the object to see the danger approaching.

Suddenly, he saw an object on the ground, something translucent, almost invisible to the naked eye, without being able to locate it precisely. His gaze could have stared at the place with maximum concentration, but he couldn't manage to do so. He wondered if his imagination was playing tricks on him when he suddenly saw it. His module started beeping at the same time, indicating that it was time for him to go back.

— Great, just when we needed to be lucky again.

He bent down to pick up the crystal, finding it as light as a feather.

— Unbelievable, how can this thing be so light?

He hadn't seen the killers approaching. They were only 30 feet away.

— It's light and it'll be lighter when you give it to me. Come on, give me that and I'll let you go.

Sad was surprised and stunned. One of the two killers approached him with his left hand outstretched to claim his due, while holding in his right hand a sort of revolver, but not like the one he usually used, when suddenly he collapsed and burst into flames. Sad was paralyzed and stunned by what had just happened. He was coming out of his trance when the second killer, who looked surprised, opened his mouth to ask what was going on.

— Damn it!

His suit started beeping. He looked at his module, which indicated « out of phase! » He looked at Sad, and knew that he only had a few seconds left to live. Sad didn't know what to do, because his module sounded louder and louder. He could make up for the lost minute by sprinting, but at the same time, he knew that the person in front of him was going to die. He put the crystal in his pocket as he approached the person frozen in front of him. He took his hand and said:

— Run!

The master didn't quite understand what was going on but noticed that the beeping of his module was lighter. And he didn't wait for him to say that again. He dropped his titanium revolver and started running hand in hand with one of the people he was supposed to shoot. They ran breathlessly, they ran for their survival. If one of them fell or let go of the other's hand, death would be immediate for both of them.

The inspector woke up, expected to be on a bed instead of this stone floor. Finding no one around, he realized something was wrong. He decided to turn back because he didn't have another option.
— So, Inspector, did Morpheus get the best you?
— How long was I asleep?
The question remained unanswered, as they noticed Sad running back, holding someone's hand!
— What the hell is he doing? Who's that other guy he's holding hands with?
— The real question, Detective, is why is he holding his hand?

The *nanodes* were overloaded, they could no longer synchronize and phase with each other. They lost their energy and could no longer stabilize the balance of the molecular structure. They were dying and killing their hosts in the process. They were programmed to protect the person wearing the suit and, like a faithful dog, they would sacrifice themselves for the wearer. Sad and the master knew that they would never reach their destination without a miracle, and if the miracle was to happen, it had to happen now, or they would both die charred like the other guy earlier. At least they wouldn't have time to suffer, since death would be immediate, and at the same time, strident beeps were heard on both modules to signal that the point of no return had been reached. Sad knew he couldn't do it, he had to at least save the others. He put his hand in his pocket to pick up the crystal and threw it. But taking the crystal on the run was not easy. Eventually he held it in his hands and just as he was about to throw it, the beeps faded. The crystal was providing the energy to reach the end of the tunnel.
They literally collapsed when they arrived, dropping the crystal which slid to Coldi's feet. They were out of breath. They felt like their

bronchial tubes were on fire, and their skin was stuck to the damn suit, as if it was not attached to their body.

— I gotta get this thing off, help me get this thing off!

— NO! Not at all! Don't remove anything, don't move... If you take anything off, you'll die!

— But the module's red, you told us to remove it immediately if it turned red.

— And now I'm telling you to keep it on. And don't move.

— But I'm...

— Shut up and don't move. Keep all your equipment, mask and gloves on.

The *nanodes* had drawn all the energy they could, so they had limited the functionality of the suit to the bare minimum, making the mask completely opaque. We could no longer discern any facial features of either the killer or Sad.

Mrs. Foxter spoke with such authority that Sad and the master didn't dare to respond.

— The rest of you stay here and rest, I'm going to see if this crystal can open that damn door. Albot, come with me, please, I have a feeling that this crystal will only work with you. I don't understand how it could have helped Sad earlier. We'll be back for you. And Inspector, keep an eye on our dear killer.

— Do you want me to get him here by holding his hand?

— No, with this.

She handed him a gun, that was in the bag she was carrying.

CHAPTER XIV: The Door

The small group walked towards the door that refused to open. They were hopeful that the crystal Sad had retrieved would be able to open the damn door, or else they would be stuck in that tunnel for a long time, without food nor water.

When they arrived at the door, Mrs. Foxter placed the crystal in front of the module that was supposed to be the locked. But nothing happened. She insisted, turning the crystal all around, but nothing happened. The door stayed closed.

— Maybe this crystal is broken or discharged from the tunnel?

— Or maybe it's not the key to open that door.

— Can I have my crystal back?

— Yes, of course. There you go.

She desperately handed it to Albot, and as the crystal touched the boy's hand, it became opaque for a second, before regaining its translucency. No one had noticed the change, except Albot, who felt a slight tingling in his fingertips, which immediately made him look at his hand and notice the brief change.

— Did you see that?

— What?

Neither Mrs. Foxter nor the others had noticed that the crystal had changed.

— Well, the crystal became opaque for a second.

— What do you mean? This crystal is translucent, I don't have any information about whether it can change color or not!

She had said it in a rather agressive way, which gave her the chills.

— I'm sorry, maybe it was just my imagination. But I felt a little tingling in my fingers, I...

Mrs. Foxter turned around and looked at him.

— A tingling sensation?

Detective Colmart had just appeared behind them.

— Maybe this crystal is connected to Albot, and when it's in contact with him it regenerates or unlocks? But I don't know anything about technology. I can barely even use my toaster.

— It's not a silly remark, Commissioner. I'm sorry, Albot, I got carried away with the frustration of not being able to open that door. I talked to you as if it were your fault.

But the inspector, who didn't appreciate Mrs. Foxter's little spike of intelligence said :

— I'm a detective, not a commissioner, Mrs. Foxter. And that is because of you, as you may recall.

— I think the statute of limitations has expired. And you're not going to dwell on this episode for the rest of your life. You were just a fuse, that's all. I've got my conscience to myself.

— And I'm holding a grudge against you. But like any good little soldier, I'm at your command once again. And there's a good chance that, this time, I'll be a traffic officer when we get back...

Albot felt a slight discomfort in the silence that had just settled in.

He decided to bring back the conversation to the main problem they were facing:

— I think we're all in the same boat. Do you mind if I try?

— That's what I was going to suggest.

Albot presented his crystal in front of the module. At first, nothing happened. Then, they heard a small beep, followed by a jacking sound and a slight squeaking. And the door opened!

— You didn't even have to say « Open sesame. »

That was the first good that had happened in a while, and they were hoping luck would finally be on their side.

— Well, here we go.

— What do you think is inside?

— Let's go in and see.

As soon as they went through the door, a light lit up the corridor, which led to a second door.

— No, not another door!

— I think it's an airlock. The first door needs to be closed, so that the other one can open.

— What if it's a trap? What if we're going to get stuck here, in this hallway?

— I don't think we have much choice, we need to move on. And I don't see a skeleton in this hallway anyway.

— There's something I failed to tell you about the combinations.

— What, that they self-destruct?

— No, but they can be stopped or put on standby. To recharge them, there are only three options. Either with our body heat, more precisely by the heat released for our body, and therefore with the energy we release. Or thanks to photosynthesis: here, there is not a lot of sunlight, and apparently these lights do not produce any. Last but not least, with the magnetic field ; but the one in the tunnel is not very suitable for the moment. To put it in a nutshell: if we don't find food and drinks within the next twelve hours, we won't have any energy left, and therefore we won't be able to return.

— That's what we call jumping out of the frying pan into the fire.

— Let's not waste any time, then. I'm going to go get Sad and our guest, the killer, before we go any further. Wait for me here, I'll be quick.

Detective Colmart walked away to go pick up his colleague and their guest. Mrs. Foxter and Albot went out into the hallway to wait outside for the inspector to come back. And the door closed immediately.

— I hope the crystal can open the door again.

The inspector returned about 30 minutes later, with Sad holding the master at gunpoint. Albot was tired, and he was starting to miss the pain medication.

— Are you all right, Albot? Are you feeling ok?

— To be honest, not really. I'm having a little bit of a fling. When we left, we forgot to take my meds.

— What can we do?

— Not much, I'm afraid. Unless either of you have any painkillers? I'd be down for an aspirine.

— Too bad the new firmware for the nanodes is not ready yet, we would have been able to help you. What are we waiting for? Let's go in. Perhaps we can find something inside that will make you feel better.

Albot placed the crystal back on its base, and the door opened. The small group entered the corridor, which lit up again. They walked towards the second door. Once again, Albot placed his crystal on the pedestal embedded in the wall. The first door closed, and the light went out right away. They were in complete darkness.

— Tap twice on your right temple, please.
Immediately, the mask balanced the lack of light.

— It's on night mode, some sort of infra-red light. It allows you to move around in the dark.

— And what do we do now, grumbled the inspector. Besides acting like bats ?

— Bats move following the radar waves, and not thanks to infra-red lights, Albot said.
Mrs. Foxter giggled, pretending to cough.

— I often go to sleep while watching late night shows about animals, and their lives. So I don't car much about bats and owls, or any other animal that can move around at night. However, i'm interested in any animal that could open this fucking door.

— Let's just stay calm, Detective, and wait a few minutes.

— Why should we wait? It's pretty clear, though, that this fucking door won't open with this fucking trivet!

— Let's just go back up where we came from.

— Albot, open the first door for me, please.

— Yes, of course, Detective. What's going on?

— Let's just say I'm a bit claustrophobic, and being in the dark and in a hallway that leads to nothing is a bit stressful.

Albot approached the crystal to the wall base, but nothing happened.

— Shit, what now?

— I don't get it!

The master, who had remained silent the whole time, coughed to draw everyone's attention.

— What's wrong with you? Do you also suffer from claustrophobia?

The master answered with a silence. It was his own technique of differentiation, to show that he was the dominant one in the group. This technique, used to deal with humans and any kind of crisis, could calm people down, and get their attention. When he spoke calmly, everyone was attentive and focused:

— This is a double door, called an Élanys door. These doors have a distinctive feature: they can only be opened with two crystals. Two doors, two crystals. In order to open the doors, the crystals must be placed on their base, very precisely. That's why this corridor is so long and so dark : it prevents any attempt of a break-in by only one individual.

— But why didn't you tell us that before we came in? You're trapped just like us!

— Because you wouldn't have listened to me, and you would have thought that I was trying to keep you out. That's typical human nature. You're too complicated, you're too narrow-minded.

— Killing people in cold blood, without any reason, without any summons, without provocation, how do you call that?

The master did not answer the question, and kept going with his explanation:

— I didn't leave. If I came in with you, it's because I wanted to get to know you.

— What do you mean, « i didn't leave »?

— Yes, my suit has been working just fine for a little while now. I could have left you a long time ago. I also could have shot you down or come back with other men. But I owe you my life. And I always pay my debts. So I came in with you, to help you get into that room.

— And you expect us to believe you, after killing all those people in the hospital? And after shooting Albot and Gustav?

— You can chose to believe me or not. In exactly five minutes, I'll be out of here. So you're going to have to listen to me carefully, or you're going to be stuck here. It's up to you.

— Please explain.

— Mrs. Foxter and Mr. Albot each have a crystal. But Mr. Albot's crystal is different: it's the only one that has the ability to open both doors.

However, since you won't be able to use it simultaneously during the split second you'll be given, you'll never get out of here.

— And what do you suggest?

The master paused again, as if he wanted to prepare them for what he was about to say.

— We're listening, Sad insisted.

— You're gonna have to trust me, and trust me with the crystal...

— Are you mad, the inspector raved. You've been looking for it for so long, you even followed us to get it back. You killed people to get it back. And now you want us to give it to you? You should stop believing in Santa Claus.

— Let him finish.

— You have the right to be suspicious. I too would be suspicious if I were you, but you don't have much choice. I can also leave you and come back in a few days to pick up from your bodies.

A religious silence reigned in this corridor. That's when Mrs. Foxter decided to speak up:

— Unfortunately, he's right. We're stuck here, and we have no other way out.

— But how do we know he's not gonna leave with the crystal? We just stand here, way and see?

— Look, my suit is working just fine, but there's still one function that hasn't been fully restored yet. It's the environmental registration system. All my gestures and actions can be verified by my controller when I get back. What will happen in the control room may kill me, so what the heck.

Albot approached the master and handed him the crystal without saying a word. The master took the crystal, approached the first door, placed it in the pedestal, and typed on a dial he had on his wrist. Then he calmly moved towards the second door and proceeded to the same operation. He looked at them, nodded his head and disappeared.

— What do we do now?

— Do we shoot ourselves in the head right now, or do we just sit here and wait to die?

— Let's just wait a few minutes, please.

They saw the master reappear a minute latter in front of the first door, and a few seconds later the second door opened. And the crystal remained on the pedestal.

— I'm going to need someone to explain to me what just happened, because I'm completely overwhelmed by all of this. Especially since this guy is acting like Houdini again!

CHAPTER XV: The Basics

The small group moved to the room behind the second door. When they entered, a slight light illuminated the room, but not completely; they were still in darkness.

And after the fourth visitor had crossed the threshold, the door closed immediately. A white and smooth wall had replaced the door. Not the slightest gap could be seen. Mrs. Foxter had tried to keep the door open, but unsuccessfully.

— Here we are, now! I hope there's a warm welcoming committee and no killers waiting for us.

They all looked at each other. They wondered what to do now. What were they supposed to do, now that they were in? What were they supposed to find, or do next?

— Let's not split up, let's stick together, we never know what could happen.

By reflex, the inspector took his weapon.

— The lighting's not great, they must have forgotten to pay the bills.

— Surely there's a switch somewhere?

— I'll buy a beer to the first one who finds it. Except if that person is you Albot, you'll get a lemonade...

They visited each room, one after the other, without finding a living soul. The first room, the one they entered, was oval. There were four distinct areas, with four entrances. This oval room, where they were now, looked like a living area with tables, a kind of kitchen, with chairs, a screen...

A second room, divided into a double sleeping area for men and women, consisted of a dozen bunk beds with showers and toilets. Then there was a working area, with computers and tables. Lastly, an exercise area, with various devices such as bicycles and treadmills.

— It's like being in an orbital station.

— What do you mean?

— A while ago, I watched a program about the international orbital station that is above our heads. And they had the same concept of areas, only narrower, of course. All we need now is a laboratory, and we'll be fully equipped.

— I think that's all there is. There's a door with an airlock at the bottom in the working space. It's a bulletproof glass door. Never seen anything like it.

— Anyway, I'm waiting for someone to pinch me so I can wake up. I'm completely overwhelmed by what's happening and everything we've been through. I'm going to have a hard time writing a report on what we've been through without my superiors sending me to the asylum.

— I'm still wondering if I didn't die in that ravine and if all of this is real or not.

— We're all tired, we're all hungry and thirsty, and we would all love a nice shower. I think we'll be safe for a while.

— Yes, but is there any food here?

They all looked at each other and then began to look for something that looked like a kitchen. But they found absolutely nothing...

— Now we're in trouble. It's bad, so bad.

— And there's not even tap water, or water in the toilets and or in the showers.

— Anybody got any ideas?

Silence was their only reaction, which wasn't very auspicious. Everyone sat down to reflect on the situation.

— What the hell is this place?

— No idea, and I have never heard of it.

— We're screwed, like rats.

— Look, let's try to get some sleep for a few hours. I guess we'll be able to think clearly afterwards.

Albot had trouble falling asleep. He pictured rats used in laboratories. His imagination got wild : he imagined these poor beasts and their life within the laboratories. Then his imagination wandered to the orbital station and the people working up there. He felt pretty confused, and yet felt like he was close to understanding everything, but he couldn't quite get there. And what exactly was this crystal? What was its purpose, apart from opening doors? He finally fell asleep after his tired brain finally shut down.

A few hours had passed when he was gently shaken.

Mrs. Foxter was standing over him.

— Good morning, Albot. Did you sleep well? I'm sorry to wake you up, but we are all awake, and we are trying to think and understand how to get out of this place.

— In three words... hunger, dirt and pain.

— Let's try to think about what we can do. To sum up : we are in this underground place, we do not know where, with no way out, no food, no water and no means of communication. It seems to me that the most appropriate word to describe this kind of situation is death!

Albot was as realistic as the others, but he refused to believe he was going to spend the rest of his life here.

— There has to be a solution. I can't believe this trip is going to end here.

— And do you have an idea?

— I'm trying to be consistent. I think it's kind of basic. And I think this base is right there, waiting for us to find it.

— And how do you think we're going to find it? A genius idea would be nice.

— It's like a switch, to turn on your computer or the lights in your house. You have to press it.

— We looked everywhere... And there's nothing.

— Let's think about this. So far, what has been used each time?

— The crystal!

— So I think the crystal is once again the key.

— That's not stupid. But how do you use it?

— Look for a pedestal or something to hold it in.

Everyone started looking everywhere, in every room and on every wall. But didn't find anything. There was absolutely nothing. An hour went by, and they still hadn't figure it out.

They all found themselves back in the living room together again, looking disconcerted.

— I didn't find anything, Mrs. Foxter admitted.

— Nothing here either, Sad added.

— Nada, Colmart ended. What do we do now?

Albot started thinking. His brain was boiling. He could almost feel smoke coming out of his skull. At that moment, the watch they had on their wrist, which was linked to the suit, changed color.

— Ouch, not good at all. If we take off our suits, we'll freeze to death in a few hours.

— The temperature here is close to 86 degrees, in Fahrenheit.

— From cold, hunger or whatever. Why does it matter? Death is death.

That's when Albot noticed some sort of sign on the ceiling, right next to the front door. By reflex, he looked at the floor, and noticed the same sign.

— What did you see?

— Mrs. Foxter, could you lend me your glasses, please? The ones you used in the bomb disposal room.

Mrs. Foxter handed him the glasses. He got up and walked towards the signs, putting the glasses on. He took the crystal out of his pocket and approached it to place it in order to make the two signs touch. He let go of the crystal, and the crystal remained in its place without moving, as if it was floating in the air.

They immediately heard a small electronic beep. And the lights were immediately switched on in all the rooms. Their mouths were all dry from leaving them open. They didn't know what to say nor think.

— But how did you...?

— Damn it! Now you're bluffing me. How did you figure it out?

— I don't know. Everything's white here, and clean. I thought: « What the hell is that messy thing on the ceiling? » We were looking at the walls and the objects, but we weren't looking up. I remembered what Mrs. Foxter's had said in the anatomy room, about looking at the ceiling.

— Okay, now the lights are on.

— And the heater as well, apparently, Mrs. Foxter added.

— And the water, said the inspector, who had flushed the toilet.

— What about the...

At the same time, a kind of hologram of a human form, and more precisely a female form, appeared. And began her speech:

— Welcome. I will be your companion during your stay. You may call me Voira, that stands for virtual organic intelligence reality augmented. I'm here to help you, and to answer your questions and needs. But know that at the end of your stay here, all of you, without exception, must pass a test, otherwise you will all be eliminated.

— What the hell is that? Where the hell are we?

— I will answer each of your questions based on the answers I have in my knowledge base. It's a fairly large and constantly evolving database.

— Voira, where are we?

— Let's start from the top. First, go to your quarters and remove your suits, they're of no use here. You can also drop all your items, weapons included. They're not allowed in here.

— You're delusional kiddo. Do you really think that I'm going to let you keep my .35?

— Sir, you're completely safe here. You're not in any danger.

— And what if I refuse? What are you gonna do to me? Run me through the body like a ghost? You're a simple computer program, and you're made of light. And I don't know you, and I don't trust you.

No one had time to react to what the inspector just said. Everyone knew that he was not entirely wrong, but also that he was not quite right.

— I'm sorry to insist, but if you don't obey immediately, I'll be forced to leave you.

— And what will that do?

— Well, if I leave you, you'll be right back where you started. But I will be forced to declare this place as compromised, and therefore destroy you. And i'll do that by cutting off the oxygen supply. In addition to that, and to speed up the process, I'll suck this one out so that you can die quickly.

They all looked at each other, not sure if it was an upward warning or a real threat.

— Look, we got off on the wrong foot. The way I see it is that we don't have much of a choice. We should do what Voira wants us to do. Anyway, what else could we do?

— All right, all right, Mrs. Foxter. Let's obey this HAL.

— Did you hear that, Voira? I think we can put an end to this misunderstanding.

But Voira did not answer. Everyone started to get worried.

— Voira! Voira! Are you still there?

— Answer us, please. We apologize for this misunderstanding.

— What now? Do you expect me to apologize to a machine?

— Look, detective, I think this machine, as you describe it, is not quite like the machines you're used to. It's not a computer like the one you have at home.

— Okay, I'm sorry I got carried away.

The hologram reappeared immediately.

— Shower and dress yourself with the clean clothes you'll find in the drawers. Then you will take turns going to the area you have called the laboratory.

— To do what?

— You will take turns going to this area, no questions asked. I'll explain when the time comes.

— Can't we eat something before we start? It's been a little while now since we swallowed anything.

— The established order of things, even if it doesn't align with what you were expecting, is the order I am asking you to follow and respect.

The inspector slowly turned to Albot to discreetly whisper something in his ear :

— I think she's mad at us.

— At you! That's because of you.

The inspector didn't dare to open his mouth again, and kept a low profile.

— We can now begin. You may go. The sooner this is over, the sooner we can talk and the sooner you can eat.

They were all too tired to object or refuse the given orders, so they all went to their sleeping area without saying another word.

CHAPTER XVI: Non-Cartesian Choices

They were surprised to see that the resting area had been completely remodeled. The layout of the room had radically changed: they now each had a small room that closed with a sliding door, with a bed, a table, a sort of computer whose mode of operation had yet to be defined, and a small wardrobe with clothes apparently their own size.

— But how is this possible? Where the hell are we?

— Maybe there are little green goblins working around the clock in the basement?

Sad had smiled at the joke, which didn't mean he wasn't worried. Such things couldn't exist in their time, there must have been a coherent explanation for all of it! The suits, the airlock, Voira, and now this room that had completely changed in a matter of minutes. It was all out of the ordinary.

They had settled in the new place, which was supposed to be their room, had showered and got dressed. Their old clothes and objects had been placed in a sort of white cube that had remained open and placed in a corner of the room. It automatically closed down once all their stuff had been placed inside.

They were all clean as a whistle, and had returned to the main area.

— What do we do now, Voira? Can we get something to eat?

— I'm sorry, but that's not going to happen for now. First, you all must pass the different tests that are in the laboratory, which is located in the working area. I'm using the same terms you used when you visited this place, so that you can find your way around easily.

— But what for?

— I'm going to model your body, check your health, take a few samples, and, depending on the results, I will submit some observations. But first of all, I have to ask you to take the little pill that is in your bathroom.

— What do you mean? What is it?

— I detected *nanotriaminums* in your bodies. You need to discharge them.

— But if we do that, we won't be able to use our combinations anymore, so we won't be able to leave.

— I'm only asking you this as a courtesy. I could immediately destroy them if I wanted to, and that would result in your immediate death.

— Once again, you're forcing us to do something without any valid reason.

— Just do what I ask you to do.

— And how would these nanothings come out? From the top, or from the bottom?

Mrs. Foxter couldn't hold back a smile. But the question wasn't a stupid one.

— Once swallowed, the pill will take effect within 30 minutes. During these thirty minutes, you will need to stay in bed. I want to be as transparent as I can with you : before you throw up, you're gonna be in a lot of pain. That pain is due to the removal and the de-merging of the *nanotriaminums* that have been placed in different parts of your body. That's why I didn't give you any food. The pain is a little less important if your stomach is empty. As I told you before, there's an order for everything.

Having no other option, they headed back to their resting place. They all felt very anxious. They were holding the pill in the palm of their hand, and were very reluctant to put it in their mouth.

Mrs. Foxter was the first one to do it, followed by Albot, Sad, and finally Detective Colmart. Then, everyone went back to their bed, nervous about the pain they were going to deal with.

Albot was the first one to stand up : for him, the pain was sudden and agressive. The injuries he had from the accident were amplified. He could barely stand when it was over, and collapsed on his bed. His body had started to tingle, his body hair stood on end, and then he had spasms. He had writhed in pain, feeling like there was a fire inside his body, but shaking because he was wold at the same time.

Usually, vomiting is very painful, but the feeling of every *nanotriaminum* being released from his cells was like pins someone would get under your skin. Except now, it was like those pins came from the inside.

What Albot had vomited was some kind of colorless fluorescent paste that was wiggling all over the place. And once it was all out, the dough disintegrated in front of him.

Each one of them went through the same traumatic experience, and they weren't going to do it again anytime soon. They were all exhausted and collapsed in their beds without saying a word.

They once again lost track of time, and were woken up by Voira's voice.

— It's time to wake up and move on to the next step.

— Can't we eat something first?

— Normally, no. But you will find protein bars on the common room table. It should help you feel a little better.

They all ate their bar as if it was their last meal on earth.

— Completely flavorless, but not too bad. Anyway, it calmed my stomach down a bit, said the inspector.

— I hope we are going to get something more substantial soon, with a bit more taste.

— All right, let's get this damn test started and get it over with!

The hologram didn't react. Voira was frozen in the middle of the room, like a statue, but half transparent.

— I guess we can continue the protocol now. Please walk towards the area you call the « working zone ». You will then enter the room located inside that area. This is not a laboratory, as you might have imagined, but a medical room. You will find four cabins, where you'll get settled. Don't worry, Mr. Colmart, even if you suffer from claustrophobia, you'll instantly fall asleep when you're inside. You won't have time to worry about anything.

— I still don't understand why we have to take all these tests...

— All your questions will be answered after you passe the tests.

They headed for that famous room.

— I feel like a prisoner walking down the death corridor.

— Let's not exaggerate, we've had an excellent last meal.

They laughed.

Voira was observing them and did not understand their behavior. She never had to deal with such undisciplined candidates before. She didn't understand their reluctance or curiosity. Usually, candidates knew what was going to happen to them. They all volunteered! Maybe someone had sent these four candidates to evaluate her? Her brain, made out of quantum nanoprocessors was, for the first time, facing a dilemma. She was as lost as the candidates. So she just kept going with her usual schedule.

She once though about killing them, when they were in the corridor leading to the entrance. But just as she was about to make that decision, they had finally managed to open the second door. Then, even though they had been slow to start the process with the crystal, they had once again found the boot system on time. And now she was starting to have serious doubts about them.

Some of those systems were working on these digital reflections while the others were working on the various tasks, such as those related to the maintenance of life in the passenger compartment, to the tests and the candidates' results, to the energy management, and the protocols for *nymphalic* reconstruction of the passenger compartment.

— Voira! The door to the second room is closed! Can you open it?

— Yes, of course, please come in and take a seat.

They all laid in their cabins, which were completely transparent, and made out of a material that looked like glass or crystal but was quite comfortable. The bottom base, which was hard at first, had immediately embraced their morphology like a shape memory mattress. They instantly fell asleep after laying down. They hadn't had time to think. They were at the mercy of a machine that had the power of life or death over them.

The first phase consisted of scanning and modeling them. During the second phase, the machine took samples of their skin, their spinal cord, their blood, and their bones. The third and final phase was to check their health and to fix any problem that may be reported in the results of the second phase. Phase two had highlighted problems on each candidate, which had never happened before: they must have been evaluating her.

She proceeded to remove a cancerous tumor from Mrs. Foxter. She blocked and corrected an orphan disease that would have declared itself within the next two years on Detective Colmart, and healed

Sad's brain injuries, who would have suffered from Alzheimer in the next few months. However, the problem with Albot seemed more complicated, but repairing most of his fractures and contusions was rather easy. His eye, on the other hand, was a bit more complicated to fix. She'd have to work on both eyes at the same time, and modify some rebuilding genes, which could be risky and result in some changes. She was hesitant.

Three of them woke up, while Albot was still asleep in his sarcophagus. They were completely dizzy, and their mouths were dry.

— What's going on with Albot?

— Is there a problem?

— You all had problems, but none that I couldn't fix. But it's a bit more complicated for Albot, and his eyes. They require a certain amount of work, which is more complex.

Voira told them what she had found in their bodies, and what she had done to fix them.

Mrs. Foxter was speechless, and had tears in her eyes. Now that she was approaching 40 years old, she had finally some hope to have children! All the doctors had told her that it would be impossible. It was extraordinary : how could such a miracle occur? She thought she would never experience the joy of being a mother! At the Descendance, there were sometimes baby orphans, but it was still quite rare. And it wasn't the same as feeling life growing inside of you.

Sad was speechless as well, and Detective Colmart, who had begun to experience certain symptoms that were probably related to the onset of this rare and incurable disease, felt a certain relief, and the heavy weight he was carrying on his shoulders disappeared. Indeed, only a few researchers were working on these rare diseases. There weren't enough patients in the world, and so it wasn't profitable enough.

They all owed their lives to that computer.

— What about Albot?

— We'll have to wait. I put him in a semi coma, so it gives me some time to check if what I've given him works. Molecular regeneration is on point, but in his case, the operation performed on him resulted in more damage. Some of the cells were irreparably damaged. And I found and removed a *nanolium* behind his eye, which was emitting images outwards. It was placed there so that people could spy on him.

— That explains why our pursuers were always one step ahead of us!

— I was starting to wonder if we hadn't been infiltrated.

Mrs. Foxter was worried about young Albot:

— What if what you gave him didn't work?

— Well, in that case, I will have to eliminate him, replied Voira.

Everyone looked at this poor Albot, who was lying in his cabin, wondering how someone could deal with so much pain.

— You can now go back to the main area, I prepared a meal for all of you.

They were all hungry like wolves, they didn't even remember the last meal they'd eaten. But at the same time, they were really scared regarding what Voira may have cooked for them. Their fear soon dissipated. Because what they found on the table was more than acceptable. It wasn't gastronomy cuisine, but the smell coming from the kitchen was lovely. There was chicken with greens and potatoes, but also fruits, cakes and yoghurt for dessert.

— But how is this possible?

However, they were too hungry to ask questions. They came closer to the table, began to take a look at the food that was on it and started eating. They were hungry, but they couldn't stop thinking about Albot, who was still in his cabin waiting for Mother Destiny to take care of him, and decide whether he should live or die.

After this frugal meal, they all felt full, and they all felt the need to rest.

— Voira, what are the chances of Albot getting through with this, Sad asked.

— I won't be able to answer that question until tomorrow. Right now, the odds are low. There's another way to increase those odds. But I would rather use it as a last resort. By the way, it's usually not a decision I can make. It's up to the person
whether or not they accept the solution. We can discuss it after you have rested.

They all got up as the same time to go to their resting area. They were exhausted from that endless day.

CHAPTER XVII: Last Wishes

Did they all have a good night rest, or a good day rest? To be honest, they had lost their bearings a little. Because they were underground, they had no way of telling the difference between day and night. They could also lose track of time, which could be very dangerous. They needed to address the Voira situation, and understand why she called them « candidates ».

— Why do you think Voira sees us as candidates?

— I have no idea.

— Maybe we should ask her?

— What if we ask her, and she finds out we have nothing to do with the expected candidates? What do you think she'll do? It's a computer. Maybe not a computer like the ones we're used to, but she's not a human being. She has no conscience and can't really function with reason, let alone have any feelings or pity. It's just a program. A more elaborate program, but a program. So there's a good chance she'll eliminate us without giving it a second thought. I don't think its designers have succeeded in programming this kind of concept. Let's wait and see how Albot's state of health develops. Let's build up our strength and figure it out latter.

They all agreed that it would be best to wait until the Albot's healing. Breakfast was quite substantial, and they once again wondered how all this food got there.

— Voira, do you have any news about Albot's condition?

— Unfortunately, not very good ones. By removing the *nanolium*, some sort of genetic trap went off. And at the pace we're going, he won't survive more than forty-eight hours.

— And there's nothing you can do about it?

— There is one solution, but I need his approval.

— But I'll give you the approval myself! He's going to die anyway, so what's better than death?

— Sometimes people would rather die than live certain things or under certain conditions.

— What is your solution?

— This only concerns Albot. I don't have to tell you anything about it.

— She's playing the doctor-patient confidentiality card now! Her designers are really smart.

— My designers, as you call them, built me and programmed me, but my program is always evolving. I learn as I go through the experiences and choices that I need to face. I gain experience through my successes and mistakes.

— You mean you have free will?

— Let's just say that I thought of eliminating you several times since you've been here. You're very different from the people I usually work with. I still don't know if I did a good job by letting you in, since you might put the whole place in danger.

They were all in shock hearing about Albot's condition.

— But there's another problem, which I also need to talk to you about. If Albot disappears, you'll disappear as well. That's one of the reasons you can't really chose for him. Because, under those circumstances, you won't be able to make a neutral choice.

They were shocked.

— What do you mean?

— The crystal that pushed you towards this base and kept you alive will automatically be destroyed if Albot dies. It is intimately connected to him, not to say they make one. It will immediately shut down this base, and I won't even have the time to say anything. There are self-defense mechanisms that aren't related to my system. They work as a security guard, in case I become uncontrollable or I make decisions that could jeopardize the group.

— What are you going to do now?

— I'm going to wake up Albot alone, explain the problem, and tell him about the options he has. I won't be able to tell him the impact his decision may have on you, as it would probably alter his decision.

— Can we come?

— You can come and see him, but then I'll ask you to leave the room so that I can talk to him alone.

— Let's go, let's get it over with, because every minute counts for him.

They all gathered around Albot, waiting for him to wake up. He woke up about an hour after Voira launched the protocol that allows her to bring him out of the coma. He woke up a little foggy, completely blind. He panicked. He had no more pain related to the several injuries caused by the accident. He felt perfectly healthy. But he couldn't see anything anymore.

— Why can't I see anything anymore? Is anyone there?

— We're all here, and we wanted to stop by and say hello before Voira talks to you alone. She's going to explain everything, you can trust her.

Everyone approached Albot to hold his hand, give him a hug or a kiss on the forehead.

— All these marks of affection are making me angry. It almost feels like you're saying goodbye to a convict. And why can't I see anything? I feel like all my bruises are gone, except for the ones in my eyes.

— I'll explain, but first, you all have to leave, like we agreed.

Voira waited until everyone was out and closed the airlock to isolate the room.

— Tell me what's going on, Voira, because right now you're freaking me out.

Voira told him everything she had explained the others, without talking about the cristal, and the impact of his decision. She explained, in details, that the solution, once applied, would be irreversible and that it was the only way to keep him alive.

— You have just under forty-eight hours to live. And the surgery should take a few hours, with an eight-hour wait. I am sorry to rush things a little, but you have to give me your answer now. Either I shorten your suffering, or I apply what I

just explained to you.

— And what does Mrs. Foxter think about all this?

— She can't say anything, the choice is yours. And I'm asking you not to tell your friends.

— I don't understand why not.

— I'll explain the reason once you've made your choice.

She had displayed the options in a completely neutral voice, without changing her tone, in order to help him make the best choice. He was tired of all the tragedy, all the deaths, the loss of his family. And now he was blind.

— Could you give me a little half hour, please, so that I can think about it calmly. This is a life-or-death decision that can't be made on the spot. I need time to absorb everything...

— I'll give you thirty minutes, and then you'll have to give me your answer. In the meantime, I'll go back to your friends.

As a quantum computer, she could only make decisions based on logic. It was based on a fundamental law that had been
established in the past by humans. The purpose of this law was
to prevent the destruction of the human race. At the time, computers were practically non-existent, so the writers had gotten used to robotics, because it was easier to imagine novels with robots than with computers. Human beings did not have the mnemonic ability to project itself this far.

The Basic Law consisted of three main rules:

1. A program may not harm a human being or a human being's health, nor allow a human being to be exposed to any kind of danger by remaining passive.

2. A program must obey orders given by a human being, unless such orders contradict the first rule.

3. A program must protect its existence as long as this protection obeys to the first or second rule.

Voira's program was created on the basis of this fundamental law. Her program was running on a loop to try to find a solution without breaking any of the rules. But a fourth rule had been added, and it was the one that was giving her the most trouble:

4. A program must consider the largest number of humans that can be saved, unless one human can save an even greater number.

This last rule was introduced to her after the creation of the computer science quantum. Quantum computing opened up a new era, as well as new horizons, with the possibility of carrying out an almost instantaneous analysis. And in this case, it could save Albot. But if Albot refused to run away, it would condemn the others. She was facing a dilemma, knowing that Albot had to live to help its designers survive, and help her as well.

Thirty minutes had gone by. Voira went back to see Albot:

— Have you made up your mind?

— Yes, I've thought about it, over and over, and I want to get it over with. I don't have a family anymore, killers want to find me, I'm in a dead end, and what you're offering is very hard to imagine. I would like to end it, and I don't want to say goodbye to my friends. It would be too hard for me. I don't even want to hear their concerns.

And he laid down in the cabin and immediately fell asleep.

Voira projected herself into the common room, in order to tell the others about Albot's decision. She had hesitated to eliminate everyone right after Albot gave his answer: no unnecessary suffering and no questions asked. It would have been set in just a few seconds. But her program, which had acquired a certain understanding of the human kind, could not bring herself to do it.

— So, what did he decide?

— He'd rather get it over with.

— Did he give you his reasons?

— From what I understood, he misses his family. He's lonely and he doesn't see a future for himself.

They sat down, all at once.

— How much time do we have?

— About twenty-four hours.

— I never thought my life would end this way.

— Can you give us till tomorrow, Mrs. Foxter suggested.

— Now that I've told you about his decision, I don't see why not.

The three of them had dinner, like old friends who hadn't seen each other for a long time. They told each other adventures, stories about their lives, talked about their families. Voira had stepped back during the evening, to let the humans commune with each other. But time flied, and they all went to their beds.

Sad and Colmart were asleep when Helena Foxter opened Colmart's room, undressed and went into his bed. It was well into the night when Helena got up without waking up Colmart.
She showered and went to Sad's room.

She blamed herself and felt like it was her fault Colmart and Sad were in this situation. But she was also a human being, and it had been forever since she had sex with a man. When she went to her bed to rest, she felt a gleam of light, and happiness was all over her face. The same glow that could be seen on Sad and Colmart's face.
The three of them met in the living room to take the breakfast. Neither Colmart nor Sad changed their behavior around Mrs. Foxter. They both didn't know what had happened and, since they didn't want to offend one another, they feigned ignorance.
After a hearty breakfast, they addressed Voira:

— Voira, I think we're ready. How would you like to proceed?

— I th...

Voira was about to propose a solution when she was interrupted by someone attempting to access her system from the outside. This was supposed to be impossible, because her system was completely isolated and self-contained. No other system could access hers, and vice versa — except when she needed it to communicate information or elements that could prove to be dangerous to the community.

The equivalent of a red phone during the Cold War. She tried to trace the attempted attack immediately, but soon realized that it was some kind of recorded message that was addressed to Albot.

Mrs. Foxter grew impatient with the heavy silence...

— Maybe Voira will start the process without explaining anything, so we don't get scared?

— Or maybe she found a less radical solution?

But they didn't have time to consider other avenues, because Voira came back.

— What's going on, Voira?

— A major security concern I have to deal with.

— Could you explain?

— As a matter of fact, it concerns you. I thought it was an attempt to intrude my system, but ultimately, it's a message for Albot.

— You confused an attack with an email? It's not really the same.

— Let's say there's no mail here, because there's no access for the outside world. So the person managed to break into my system to deliver the message.

— It's a message for Albot? Who's it from? And what does it say?

— Can we see it?

Voira thought about it, looking through her algorithm to see if she could respond favorably to this request.

— Usually, this message could only be read in the presence of Albot. But given his condition and the time you have left, I think I can allow it.

A hologram that looked like Voira appeared in the middle of the room.

And they immediately recognized the master's image.

CHAPTER XVIII: The Passage

The master began his recorded monologue:

— I think you all recognize me. If you're listening to this message, it means that you're alive, and that you managed to get the base running. You're probably wondering why I'm sending you a message. I'm asking you to listen carefully, because you won't be able to hear it again. And it will fade as it is broadcasted.

He took a short break, so that everyone could focus on what he was about to say.

— I'm taking an enormous risk in bringing you this message and the following information. When I took your crystal, to help you get into that base, mine got in touch with yours and they have communicated with one another. Your crystal is far more powerful than mine, but a fragment of information, or more precisely coordinates, have been recovered. For now, the information is encrypted, but there is a high probability that it will be decoded within a few days. These coordinates lead to the Descendance site. They want to send groups there in order to eliminate everyone and destroy everything. You must absolutely go there and convince everyone to evacuate the site. You need to find the passage: it's a room that has been closed and hidden since World War II. It will help you transfer from the site.

— It's just a guess, but I think your crystal can be used as a key for this operation. As for the evacuation, I don't know how you can proceed, but I think Albot will be able to help you. You may think it's a trap, and have trouble trusting me. I have no argument or evidence to convince you. I'll let you choose your destiny. It is unlikely that our paths will ever cross again, because they will probably send people to kill me. They must see me as a traitor.

— This message is coming to an end. I guess you must have noticed that a *nanolium* had been transplanted onto Albot. And you probably already removed it. It unleashed some kind of destructive genetic virus, what you might also call a genetic Trojan horse. I don't have a cure, and it's irreversible. But I'm going to give you the formula for a molecule capable of slowing down its effects by a day or two. This might give you time to figure out a solution. Good luck to you and above all, take care of Albot. Many lives depend on him. And don't you ever get rid of the crystal.

The message stopped dead. They were silent for a while, staring at each other, not knowing what to think. Voira spoke first:

— This situation is unusual, my calculators are looking for a solution. But the integrity of this base is compromised and I'm going to have to proceed to its destruction.

— What about us? What about Albot? We have to wake him up and give him your treatment. We don't have much time left.

— Do you think this guy said the truth in his message? Or is it just a trap to follow us to the Descendance and destroy it?

— To be honest, I think he's telling the truth. Anyway, what else do you want do? Forget that message and let us die like you planned to? Or take his message as a warning, and help as many people as possible to get away with it?

It was a dilemma with far-reaching consequences, and one that would impact many more people than their four little lives.

— Voira, what do you think of the formula he gave us to help Albor?

— It could actually save us a day or two.

— You must go against Albot's choice and administer the formula as well as your treatment. And then we will leave this base to go to the Descendant.

— The situation is getting too serious in terms of consequences. I am required to contact my designers, explain everything and let them decide what to do.

— But where are your designers?

— On the main site!

— What's that site? Where is it located? Who lives there?

— I can't answer your questions. Nor can I make a decision about Albot. I have to refer to my designers for the first time since I've been around. I will give Albot the formula that has been given to us, so we can save some time. I don't think my designers will be able to make a quick decision.

— Help us, Voira, please.

— I'll do what I can, but I can only focus on logical things. Although I am able to adapt to any situation or to make rational decisions on my own, I learn as I go, thanks to the situations I face and the experiences. And that particular situation is brand new to me. I'll leave you to it, I have to contact them.

Voira left them, alone with their thoughts.

— What do we do now, Sad asked.

— We wait, replied Mrs. Foxter.

It had been twenty-four hours since Voira had disappeared. They tried to keep their minds off things, but they as busy as they were, but they were starting to feel like time was passing slowly. The small group had been thinking about the situation and the choices that could be made, but something remained constant in their conversations: they all wanted to go back to the real world. They didn't want to be locked up in this sanitized place, and they didn't want to spend their days talking to a machine. They were hoping that Voira would come back with good news.

Voira's hologram reappeared the next day.

— Voira, there you are!

— Tell us what they have decided.

— I think it's best if he tells you himself. But first, I have to administrate you some *Symlium*.

— Some what?

— A *Symlium* is something that will help you understand the language.

— Is it like some kind of universal translator?

— I guess that's what you can call it. I'm going to attach it to your temple : that's where the cerebellum, that controls the language, is located.

— I suppose we don't have a choice?

118

— No. Settle into your respective cabins. It's only going to take a few minutes. You'll feel imbalanced and may want to vomit : these are the side effects, but they won't last long.

— All right, let's go, what are we waiting for? I don't even want ask any questions anymore.

The intervention, which lasted about thirty minutes, was simultaneously made on Helena, Sad and Colmart. They got up with a severe headache, a strong urge to vomit and the inability to stand. Their heads were spinning.

— Don't worry, in a few minutes, everything will be back to normal. Take a glass of water, it will help you. There, I think you are ready, now.

A second hologram appeared next to Voira. It was an old person, with a white beard, dressed all in white.

— Hello, I am Oerelius the fifth. I am the representative of the consul who has been chosen to come and talk to you.

Voira told me all about the issue, and the danger that you and ourselves are facing. We haven't interfered in your lives for a long, long time. And we don't want to change that, but apparently we don't really have a choice.

The *Symlium* was working just fine. They never got the impression that the interlocutor spoke a different language than theirs.

— But who exactly are you?

— One thing at a time. And time is running out, apparently. I think the person who warned you unfortunately said the truth. You need to go to the site you call the Descendance and evacuate everyone. You must also find the room that was condemned after World War II. I've added some additional information into your cristal : the coordinates of the main site. I have a reason to believe that the cristal will bring these buildings in their original location. But it's important that you never lose this cristal, and that Albot doesn't get hurt. I don't know how, but he's the one who's linked to it. We are trying to figure it out.

— But how do you expect us to evacuate more than five hundred people?

— And how do we convince them to evacuate?

— Even if we find the hidden room, what are we supposed to do next?

— Find the room first, and then we'll work on finding a way to help you evacuate everyone.

— But maybe Albot will have an idea?

— While we were talking, Voira launched the protocol on Albot. I hope he will accept the situation, because it might come as a shock to him.

— But what the hell is this damn solution that Voira was so reluctant to give him?

— He suffered a massive destruction of his genome. Under normal circumstances, he should already be dead. We need to rebuild his genome, his genetic heritage is very important. But in order to do that, we're going to give him a new kind of pill. The *Femtriaminum*, and not the *nanotriaminums*. This new technology is still being developed : we are going to give him a modified version of it. But since it is difficult for these *Femtos* to manage that much information, we're going to integrate the equivalent of Voira in his brain, which will stabilize and control all the *Femtos*.

— Now I understand why you were so reluctant. I wouldn't want to be the first one to break the news to him when he wakes up. You know what, Albot? A computer has taken control of your brain. And by the way, when you have children, if you survive, of course, well, they'll have a genome that's slightly modified. What a life! Now I understand why he chose to die.

— We didn't explain anything to him, he refused the solution without knowing all the details.

— I'll leave you to it.

— How can we contact you?

— I'll come back as soon as you place the crystal in the hidden room of the Descendance. Then, and only then, you'll understand.

And the consul's representative disappeared. At the same moment, a sound of explosion made the speaker vibrate.

— Shit, what's going on now, shouted the inspector.

— We're under attack. I'm initiating the self-destruction mode, Voira said.

Voira added in a neutral yet domineering voice:

— Hurry to your beds and put on the new jumpsuits and your clothes. Take Albot's clothes and suit as well. And come back here to help Albot do the same. Take the crystal that is in the entrance as well.

Everyone hurried and followed Voira's recommendations. And while they got ready, the explosions kept going off and on. They all returned to the room where Albot was.

— Voira, the explosions are getting closer!

— I won't be able to hold them back much longer. I practically drifted all power from the base to protect its access. The magnetic field barrier that protects access is getting weaker.

— How much time do we have before they get into the base?

— I would say a little bit less than an hour.

— How are we going to get out of here?

— Take care of Albot, he's waking up. Prepare him, and explain the situation.

Albot was starting to emerge from his sleeping state. He was shivering, had a terrible headache and some nauseas. He felt weak. But he could see again.

— What's going on? Why am I still alive? And what about the pain in my head? Voira, what did you do to me?

— Albot, we don't have much time for a debate and to explain everything in greater detail. The situation is serious: we have been forced to break your vows. You can judge us later. For now, we need to get out of here. A lot of lives depend on us.

— We're going to help you get dressed.

Sad and Colmart helped Albot get into his new suit.

— We're ready, Voira. What do we do now?

You swallow these new pills that are on this table. These pills are far more advanced than the ones you had when you got here. They're also going to work quicker. You, Albot, don't need it. You already have what you need.

— What do you mean?

— Not now, we don't have time.

They heard a loud explosion, that made the whole base crumble.

— It's over, they're in!

Mrs. Foxter handed the crystal to Albot.

— Here, Albot, take your crystal back.

They heard footsteps approaching their zone. The soldiers were shooting on the bulletproof glass door.

— Voira, if you have a plan, now would be a good time to tell us about it.

— I think it's the right time, we can go now.

— What do you mean, « we »? Are you coming too? How?

A silence followed, which couldn't mean something good was going to happen. She did not answer.

— When I'll open the path, you'll have to run. This passage will lead you to the surface. Your suits will protect you from outside conditions. This base, as well as the passage you are about to use, will be immediately destroyed.

— But where does this passage lead us?

They didn't have time to get an answer. They took their things and rushed into a passage that had appeared at the back of the room. It was some kind of black hole, where they couldn't see anything. They went in without thinking, and without asking any question. The passage closed immediately behind them. Before the passage had fully closed, a small capsule, that was about the size of a pen cap, with a kind of blue transparent tube, fell at their feet.

Albot picked it up.

— What the hell is this?

— I have no idea, but I think you should drop it.

— But where have we landed?

CHAPTER XIX: The Pack

The four travelers were standing and looking around them, trying to figure out where they were. But they couldn't see anything, except snow as far as the eye can see.

— But where are we?

— That's a good question. Where did Voira drop us?

All of a sudden, Albot froze and fell to the ground, shaking.

— Shit, what the hell is going on?

Despite the fact that he was wearing a hoody, they could see that his eyes were rolling. A small voice was heard in each of their heads.

— Don't worry, it's normal. It will pass.

— Voira, is that you? But how can this be possible?

— The little computer that was transplanted into Albot's skull, well… it was me. It was the only way to save him. No other machine could process that much information. The *Femtriaminum* is too unstable for now. I need to be able to stabilize him from the inside. But I'm going to need some time. These seizures are due to the modifications, and the reassembling, of his genetics. I already made the main modifications, but a few are still in a terminal phase. I have to compensate so that his body can cope, and so we can avoid rejection.

— How long is this going to take?

— I don't know about that. I'm going to go through it phase by phase, so that he doesn't run out.

— But how did you get in our heads?

— I'm using Albot's combination as a transmitter. The combinations can communicate with each other. And the *Symlium* that I gave you allows the protocol used to be transcoded.

They didn't quite understand Voira's explanation, but the important thing was that they now had an extra ally to help them get out of this nightmare.

— That doesn't tell us where we've landed?

— We're in the tundra, in Russia.

— How is that possible?

— The passage you've been going through is a kind of temporal gate. This passage makes it possible to go from point A to point B, as long as we have the correct coordinates in space-time.

— I don't understand, we teleported, like in a sci-fi movie?

— No, not really. I've opened a passage with coordinates that were communicated to me in case of an emergency. Just like the tunnel that you walked through to get to the base, it's one of the first gates to have been created. There are five of them on this planet, and now we're down to four, since I destroyed one. These coordinates work like a GPS, except they're on the scale of the universe. In addition to those space coordinates, it's also necessary to consider the ones that are on a time scale, which is based on the perpetual motion of the stars. The earth is a star that is constantly moving. It is thus necessary to calculate the coordinates with the right parameters, otherwise you'll end up in space or inside a mountain. The easiest way to do it, is to go to a place and memorize the contact information.

— And you don't have any other coordinates?

— My knowledge base hasn't been updated with other contact information, for security reasons. And that's why I can't create another passage out of here.

— And that capsule, which came after us, is it yours?

— No, it's a transmission capsule. Some kind of marker for our pursuers. They must have thrown it before the passage closed and everything explodes.

— Does that mean they can follow us?

— What color is the capsule?

— It was blue. Wait! It's red now.

— Our pursuers now have the coordinates...

— How long until they get here?

— They need to analyze the destination, process the coordinates, and check the accuracy of the data. It might take a few days. Maybe two, maybe three.

They hadn't fully understood Voira's explanations, but they were sure about one thing : they were stuck in a white desert. With chasers who could find them any day now.

They had to deal with extremely low temperatures, and their street clothes weren't really adequate for this type of meteorological condition. It's a good thing they had their suits on, made out of *nanodes*, otherwise they'd all have frozen to death a long time ago.

Albot was slowly coming back to himself, the tremors had faded, but he still had a headache.

— What happened? Why am I hearing Voira's voice in my head?

They looked at each other, not knowing where to start. How could they explain that a quantum computer had been partly transplanted in his brain?

— Voira, please tell us which way to go. Albot, we'll give you all the details along the way.

— Head north, and you should reach the M8 road within a three to four hours walk. Then you'll have to pray for a vehicle to pass by, and that the driver agrees to take you to Severodvinsk. There's a small airfield over there.

— I can't imagine the look on the guy's face when he'll see us on that road, in our street clothes out on the tundra, without any bags or equipment... We'll come up with some lame excuse. Come on, let's get moving.

And they began to tell and explain to Albot the latest events that had taken place with Voira's help. The explanations on what Voira had been forced to do in order to keep him alive made him crumble. The holographic visit of Consul Oerelius surprised him. And not to mention the part on the evacuation of the Descendance and the hidden room. But, after all the explanations, Albot felt completely helpless and no longer in control of his destiny.

The snow was up to their knees. They had forgotten that walking in the snow without snowshoes was almost impossible. Their clothes were completely frozen, making it difficult to move around. However, they weren't cold at all thanks to their suits, but needed to find a way to eat in order to have enough energy to go through it all.

— We've been walking for hours, and we haven't seen any road.

— Voira, when you said three to four hours of walking, were you talking about days?

— My calculations didn't take into account the difficulty of walking in the snow. You must quickly find a place to rest,
or you won't make it. I noticed that several presences have been following you for about an hour.

— Are our killers after us?

— No, they have four legs, more like a pack of wolves. They are waiting for you to get weak. There's a wood on your left, go there. I have a reason to believe there's a heating point in that direction. But I can't tell you exactly where it's coming from.
These good and bad news gave them a lot to think about.

— We're not gonna to get eaten by wolves, not after all we've been through!

They went into the woods, where they couldn't see each other clearly anymore.

— Let's switch our hoods to night mode.

— That's better, much better.

— I can see the eyes of our pursuers.

— I'll switch Albot's hood to thermal detection mode, to help us find the source of this heat.

This mode allowed him to see their environment a lot better and the heat released by their pursuers. They were about 50 yards away.
The pack consisted of about ten adult wolves. These were starting to surround them. But Albot couldn't see any other source of heat.

— Voira, were you positive about what you said when you told us to walk into the woods? Because I can't see any other heat source.

— I am positive: I've detected a thermal source, and you're probably close to it.

The wolves were now getting closer, and were apparently not scared of the humans. They were trying to sniff out the weakest one in the group, so they could attack him first.

— What do we do now?

— We gather in a circle and pick up pieces of wood.

The leader of the pack howled, and seven wolves came forward, showing their teeth and grunting. The chief stayed back, with two other wolves. One of the wolves, a grey one, attacked first. Sad broke a piece of wood on his skull, which made him immediately retreat. But two others had already made their way to Mrs. Foxter, and two others were attacking Colmart. They were swirling their poor wooden weapons in the air when the leader of the pack jumped on Albot. Nobody saw it coming.

It was a diversion, to isolate the weakest one. The fangs had closed on Albot's arm, who had the reflex to protect himself from an attack on his throat. The wolf jumped back immediately, loosing a canine on the battlefield. The other wolves stopped right away, and gathered.

— What happened, Voira?

— Your suits have the ability to become very hard, and release a high electric voltage. I hardened Albot's forearm just as that wolf was closing its fangs. And I sent him an electric shock.

— Well done, but will they come back?

— Yes, I don't think they'll give up that easily.

— What are they doing now?

The wolves had gathered and looked like they were fighting. They grunted at each other, especially the leader of the pack, which was against a black wolf that had decided to stay back during the attack. They were circling around an imaginary shape, grunting and showing their fangs. And all of a sudden, the two wolves rushed forward.

The black wolf feigned a hold at the throat and closed his fangs on the left front leg of his opponent. They heard a breaking sound, and the leader of the pack barked in pain, laying on the ground.

A new dominant male had just assumed the role of leader. The former leader emitted a bark of submission. But the new chief didn't stop there and bit his neck, ripping off a piece of his right ear. He wanted to dominate the pack by showing his fury.

— Ouch, this is getting complicated.

— I think this new chief is completely crazy.

— Look, the rest of the pack just joined them. They are about twenty now!

— Now we're in trouble.

It was now dark, and all they could see were the wolves' eyes. It's a good thing they had their suits on, which allowed them to see at night. Albot continued to look for a heating source in the woods, but apart from nocturnal animals, he couldn't see anything that might help them. The wolves had apparently gotten together. They walked towards their preys and began to surround them again.

— If you are believers, now is the time to say a prayer.

Albot was shaking like a leaf. He kept looking for the slightest heat source so they could escape from this wood when, suddenly, he thought he was dreaming.

— I see something.

— Where, Albot? Which way?

— Let's just say it's hard to show you and it's hard to estimate.

— What do you mean?

— I think it's a tree house. Very high up.

— No wonder we didn't find it in the middle of the night.

— Anyway, it's not stupid. We won't be disturbed by the wolves.

— How far away is it? Voira, can you help us?

— I'd say 550 yards away. But you're lucky, because the snow under the woods is harder and denser. You should have less problem moving around.

— But there are wolves in our way!

— We should run towards them, screaming and waving our pieces of wood at them.

— We're going to force our way. Now!

They started running, shouting and swirling what they used as weapons. The wolves seemed surprised by this change of strategy. The two wolves who stood in their way ran away, with a woodcut on their right flank. But the new leader of the pack barked and all the wolves started running behind them. The ground was more or less hard, as Voira had predicted, but there were a lot pieces of wood, branches and stones strewn across the ground. They could fall at any moment, and their pursuers would end up eating them in a matter of seconds.

They were halfway there. The wolves were right behind them, they were only a couple of meters away when Voira ordered the suits to accelerate. The wolves, who had almost caught up with their prey, were astonished. This acceleration allowed the group to get to the tree the cabin was on. They stood with their backs against the tree, with their sticks in front of them. The tree had no branches they could reach. Whoever lived up there must have cut off all the branches to make sure no one could climb.

— So what do we do now? There's no doorbell, apparently.

The wolves had just arrived in front of the tree. They were going back and forth, barking and showing off their teeth. The quartet started yelling at the cabin. Albot took a tiny rock and threw it on the cabin. Sad and Colmart did the exact same thing.

— Is anybody up there?

— There's light, and the detected heat source is from a fireplace. The leader of the pack came forward alone, probably to show the others that he wasn't afraid and that he was the dominant male.

— Voira, do you think you can do the same thing you did earlier but with the other pack master?

— Yes, Albot, but you're very low on energy. You won't be able to do it more than once. Why?

— I'm going to provoke him, and when he attacks me, I want you to do the exact same thing you did earlier. But this time, amplify the electrical discharge.

— Are you crazy, Albot? It's way too dangerous!

— We're going to die anyway if we don't do anything. If this works, it'll give us some time to figure out a solution.

He stopped the discussion abruptly, and stepped forward to face the pack master. The wolf weighed about a hundred pounds, and had a scar on the left side of the muzzle. The tip of his tail was missing. The wolf starred at him, probably surprised not to feel any fear in his small prey's eyes. Albot had the feeling it was a vicious and voracious wolf.

He wouldn't get a second chance.

The wolf jumped on Albot, who moved aside in the last second. Voira had analyzed every movement and muscle of this wolf, in order to calculate the trajectory of the jump and to be able to give the right tempo to Albot. The teenager grabbed the wolf by his right flank, and closed his arms around its neck. A huge electric shock was sent to Albot's forearm, which struck the leader of the pack.

The wolf laid on the ground, lifeless. Albot got up, half stunned. He was staggering, but was still standing. A wolf then approached him, followed by a second one. The little quartet stood there, ready to fight. But the pack approached very gently, with small groans, without any signs of aggression. They sniffed out their pack leader who laid lifeless on the ground. And emitted little cries of submission. One of them, who must have been a female, licked Albot's hand, looked at him and yelped. Then the whole pack disappeared in the woods in a matter of seconds.

— Albot, I almost peed my pants.

— Either you've got a big pair in your pants for someone your age, or you just don't care about life.

— Thank you, Voira. Even if you don't understand what that means or represent.

— All I did was help you implement your idea. I wasn't the one who faced a monster who weighed over two hundred pounds.

— We have to find a way up to climb that tree.

— Yes, for sure, and you might want to do that quickly. Because I detect, via your sensors, that your suits need to be recharged.

That's when they heard the voice of someone who had a strong Russian accent, coming from the cabin:

— Hey, you, down there, who are you?

CHAPTER XX: Christmas in the woods

The person who spoke was standing about 20 feet above them. At that distance, they guessed it was a woman in her thirties. But they weren't sure. She was pointing a gun at them. And she didn't seem to appreciate foreigners.

She spoke in Russian, but their *Symlium* translated everything simultaneously.

— Who are you? What do you want?

The problem is, they couldn't answer in Russian, since the translations only worked one way. She kept asking the same questions in Russian.

— Who are you? What do you want?

— We're in such a mess.

The four friends tried to open a conversation to reassure her.

— Do you speak French or English? We are not armed, we don't want to hurt you.

The only answer was a silence that lasted a few minutes. Minutes which allowed them to think about the situation. She eventually broke the silence by speaking in French.

— I speak a little French. Who the hell are you?

— We need help. We need to rest and regain strength.

— Where are sled dogs? Car? You cold?

She must surely have wondered about their street clothes, which were not very suitable for this region. And how could they have landed here without any transportation? They thought of a plausible and realistic answer, in order to gain her trust. Mrs. Foxter replied :

— We were on a plane, but we were forced to land in emergency. We've been walking for several hours and we're exhausted, we need to rest and eat.

— You walk around in those clothes for hours? You last maximum thirty minutes. You not telling truth. You can't live.

The discussion was getting bogged down.

— Listen. We're researchers, and we wanted to come here to test new clothing that can withstand the cold. But the batteries that feed our clothes are starting to weaken, so we need to recharge them.

— Hard to believe you.

— You can't just let us die outside your cabin!

— You have no weapons?

— No, we don't have anything on us.

That's when Albot had a new crisis, collapsing on the ground, shaking.

— What's going on, Voira?!

— I used too much energy earlier with the wolf, and I don't have enough left to deal with the *Femtos*. He needs warmth and food.

— I think we all need the same thing.

A rope ladder had just fallen down from the tree.

— I Traska, you can come up.

They didn't hesitate one bit. Sad took Albot on his shoulders, and started climbing. Colmart was holding the bottom of the ladder so it would be a bit stable. Once Sad and Albot were up, Mrs. Foxter began climbing, followed by Colmart. It took a certain time, because the scale was not very stable. But after a few minutes, they finally made it to the platform where the cabin was.

It wasn't on the tree they just climbed, or around it, as they expected it to be. But it was between five trees. Trees close enough to allow this type of construction.

The cabin must have been about 300 square feet. The branches of the trees protected the roof, thus avoiding too much weight due to the accumulation of snow. The interior was illuminated by two kerosene lamps and a fireplace.

Albot had been laid down on a sort of wooden sofa in front of the fireplace.

— I have coffee to warm you, and cookies.

— Thank you very much for your help, Traska. I'm Helena, and the friends who are accompanying me are Sad Hamler, Georges Colmart, and the teenager who's laying down is called Albot.

— I think it's funny that you introduced me with my first name, George, and not just Colmart.

Mrs. Foxter pretended she didn't hear the remark.

— Your friend Albot have what? Sick?

— It's hard to explain. He needs to get his strength back.

Even though Traska had welcomed them so kindly, and surely saved their life, they weren't ready to unpack their whole story to a perfect stranger. And she still had to be able to believe them.

— I prepare food for you. You wash next door. Hot water too.

— Do you live here alone? What do you do?

— I live with friend, and he leave to get fuel for group and food. But he not come back, me worry. We work here for
nature study.

— How long has it been?

— One year plus three months.

She pointed to a calendar hanging on the wall with days crossed out on it.

— Is your calendar up to date?

— Yes, me cross days. Why?

— If your calendar's up to date, then tomorrow night is the December the 24th. Christmas Eve.

— With everything that has happened to us, I'm completely lost in the dates.

— If, as a gift, someone could bring me back home, I would be so pleased.

The cabin consisted in a living room, a small room with a bed and a small toilet. It was very basic, but fit to live in.

— If you don't mind, I'm gonna go try your Robinson toilet.

Albot was slowly coming back to his senses. Voira, who had remained silent until now, explained Albot's state of health.

— He's doing better, but he needs to eat and rest. Don't answer me, or that person will get worried. I'm putting myself on standby.

They had dinner, talked about the rain and the weather, but never went into potentially compromising details.

— Tell me, Traska, didn't you hear our screams earlier, and the wolves?

— I hear wolves, but think they attack caribous. Up here, not hear all the noises.

And it was true : from the moment they were inside, they had the impression that the room was soundproof.

— Cabin build high for danger, and double wall for cold. Not hearing everything. You tired, I give you blankets to sleep.
They were all deadly tired and soon fell asleep, one after the other by the fireplace. They soon plunged into the arms of Morpheus, wrapped in the blankets that Traska had given them.
They were woken up in the early morning by the sun's rays, coming through the window. Traska had prepared a meal with cereal, coffee and powdered milk.

— Tell me, Traska, don't you have a way to communicate?

— Have radio, but no electricity. No petrol for groups.

— How long ago did your friend leave?

— Five days, today six days.

— Does he usually take this long?

— Him come back after three days, and one time after four days. But now I worry. Him, maybe accident or attacked by wolves.

— What are you gonna do if he doesn't come back?

— Me leave here, no electricity, no food, no possible to stay.

— How did your friend leave?

— Us have motorcycle with trailer.

— I assume you mean a snowmobile with a sled.

— Yes, snowmobile with sled.
They didn't have a good feeling about poor Traska's friend.

— Do you want to come with us? We can only leave tomorrow or the next day to make sure your friend doesn't come back.

— Me think.

— We'll wait for your answer before we leave.

— Thank you.

Sad and Colmart spent their morning chopping wood and pulling it up thanks to a clever pulley system. They both left at the beginning of the afternoon to try and chase their evening meal. Traska had lent them two guns. She had warned them that normally, in this season, the birds had already migrated.

After looking for several hours in the woods, they decided to check out those woods. The sun, at that time of the year, fell very early. And they didn't want to be in the woods once the night falls. One encounter with the wolves was enough for them and they didn't want to live that experience ever again.

The two hunters had come out of the little wood to try to find which could be the closest thing to a turkey when they stumbled upon a small group of snow geese. Geese that apparently hadn't migrated yet. This small group, about a dozen geese, was around a small and hot water source, that radiated its heat over a hundred yards, melting the snow all around. This allowed the birds to have food via roots and leaves. Santa Claus was apparently early.

They had to make sure they didn't miss their targets, otherwise they would have to say goodbye to their Christmas Eve meal. Both Sad and Colmart were focusing on targeting the animals, and they shot two big white geese. They looked at each other, with a big smile on their face, proud as peacocks.

Traska couldn't believe that they had managed to find snow geese in this season, because they normally migrate in September. She prepared the geese with wild potatoes and mushrooms. She had a tin of candied fruit and a some flour, which allowed her to prepare some sort of Christmas cake. It was a Christmas Eve they were not about to forget.

The sound of the logs burning in the fireplace and the dance of the flames comforted them. They had noticed through the window that the snow had started falling again. They joked and laughed, they tried to forget, just for the night, their doubts and their feeling of fear.

Traska gave Sad and Colmart the two rifles they had used in the afternoon as a gift. She offered Helena some sort of little
hair clip, and a retractable knife to Albot.

But they didn't have a gift to give her in return. Traska sensed the discomfort, and reassured them:

— Thank you for gift.

The four friends looked at each other, wondering what gift she was talking about:

— For beautiful wolf skin.

And she pointed to the window. Traska had skinned the leader of the wolf pack, the one Albot had electrocuted the day before, stretched his skin out to dry.

— Will make good winter cover.

All looked at each other, and suddenly laughed to tears.

It was then that Voira, who had remained silent until now, decided to wish them a merry Christmas. She addressed the four travelers:

— I wish you a Merry Christmas, although my program does not really understand what that means. My sensors tell me that you are relaxed. And that's all that matters.

— Thank you, Voira.

— Helena, I'd like to give you a wonderful gift as well.

Each of them wondered what Voira could possible give her.

— Yes, Voira, we're listening.

— Well, I'd like to congratulate you.

— Congratulate me? Why?

— Congratulate you on the baby you're carrying inside you.

Each of them was stunned by the news. Mrs. Foxter didn't understand what Voira was implying.

— Voira, I don't understand what you're saying!

Poor Traska didn't understand what was going on either, and she wondered who this Voira was.

— Excuse me, but me don't understand. Who are you talking to?

— It's hard to explain. And it's a very long story.

— You waiting for baby?

— Let's just say it's not clear. Voira, could you please explain?

— You had intercourse in the base, and this baby is the result of those intercourses. Your suit and the nanodes tell me everything regarding your health. And it turns out that your body is starting to adjust.

— But it's only been a few days. How is this possible? I can't have children.

— During my diagnosis, in the passenger compartments, I settled all your differences problems. I told you about them.

— Yes, I remember that. But I never would have imagined that it would be possible to make a baby that fast.

— What I did to heal each of you was immediate. And your ovaries were immediately fertile. And you had intercourse on the day after! However, I can't tell you right now who the father is.

Mrs. Foxter was bright red. Both men thought they could be the biological father, but they didn't know they were both considered for the job. Sad and Colmart looked at each other both suspicious. But the misunderstanding quickly came to an end when Mrs. Foxter addressed them:

— Sad, Colmart, I'm sorry. We thought we were going to die the next day. It was a way to leave this world without any regret or bitterness. I forced you to follow me, and if you had died, it would have been my fault, she said with tears beginning to run down her cheeks.

Sad and Colmart didn't know how to react to the news. Colmart was the first one to speak up:

— Helena, I understand your reaction, but I won't hold it against you. I had a lovely night, thanks to you. Any dead convict would have wished that kind of farewell.

Sad said:

— You know, I never thought I'd end my life with such a memory. You brought me peace, and I felt like I was ready to leave this the world thanks to you. This baby was conceived with love, and I can't blame you. The only thing I can do, is thank you.

Albot, who had been listening closely, was completely lost.

— I've been with you for some time now. But right now, I'm as dumped as Traska.

Mrs. Foxter explained what had happened and why she acted the way she did. And Albot couldn't believe it.

— But that means it's all because of me! If I hadn't taken the decision to leave this world, you wouldn't have to face this situation.

Voira addressed Mrs. Foxter:

— Mrs. Foxter, I still don't really understand how the human mindset works. My intelligence analyzes, calculates and interprets information. And I'm going to keep educating myself thanks to you. Now that I see how you all reacted, maybe I should have told you about the baby another way. I sometimes lack of judgment and sensitivity. Unfortunately, my program doesn't have these properties, which only belong to the human species. Please forgive me.

Traska got up to go outside. They all wondered why she would go out with this weather.

— Is she gone?

— I have no idea.

— She came back two minutes later with a bottle in her hand.

— What is it, Traska?

— It's better when cold. We celebrate baby, with Russian vodka. *Za vache zdorovie*!

They all looked at each other and laughed. And said, in unison:

— *Za vache zdorovie*!

CHAPTER XXI: The ambush

The day after, everyone went about their business. The group wanted to help their host as best as they could, either by chopping wood, by hunting or helping her fill the water tank, in order to show their gratitude.

The hot water system was simple, but effective. The chimney served as a boiler, via a clever system of pipes that passed under the fireplace. Moreover, the weight of the chimney, with its stones, seemed to be incompatible with this high cabin. But by looking closer at it, they noticed that the weight of the chimney sat on a sixth tree, which allowed it stay still, otherwise the chimney would have fallen through the floor.

Voira kept sending messages, inviting them to leave. Their combinations were now fully loaded and Albot was in good condition to travel. She didn't understand the human concept of being grateful. Mrs. Foxter agreed with Voira, but now that she knew about the baby, she only wanted them to feel safe. And that perched cabin somehow reassured her.

It was Albot who initiated the debate:

— We can't stay here forever, Mrs. Foxter. We should head to the Descendance, to help the people who are there.

— You're right, but waiting another day won't put them any more danger.

— Yes, it will. From what you've told me, our pursuers will soon decrypt the coordinates. It's just a matter of time. And we're still pretty far from our destination. We must leave.

Colmart, who had come back from hunting and had only heard the last bits of the conversation, agreed:

— Albot's right. We have to leave first thing in the morning.

— But Traska's not ready to leave.

— We can't risk waiting for our executioners here. We're putting her in danger.

— I'll ask her again. Either she stays, or she comes with us.

Traska opened the cabin door at the same time. Mrs. Foxter told her, in a soft and calm voice:

— Traska, we can't wait any longer, we have to leave. Our friends are in danger, and we have to warn them. Also, there are people chasing us and they might find us here. What do you want to do?

— Me think, and me think my friend is in trouble. Me come with you to town to see where he is.

— All right, we'll leave tomorrow morning at sunrise.

— I give you clothes for travel.

Traska had already provided them with clothes as soon as they arrived, since their street clothes weren't very suitable for the extreme temperatures of this region. Even if their suits could protect them, a layer of extra heat would save them energy. The new clothes were meant for cold weather, and were in fact much more suitable for travel. They were a bit too big for Albot, although they belonged to Traska. They had discussed with Voira the direction they needed to take to reach
the nearest town. But Traska wanted to take the path his friend must have borrowed to get home. It would extend their journey, but it was still reasonable. Voira obviously disagreed, but the decision was theirs to make, and not a computers, no matter how sophisticated it was.

Traska provided them with backpacks, snowshoes, guns, two tents and food for two or three days. They left at dawn. Traska was sad to leave her cabin behind, but she could feel something had happened to his friend.

At least, there was one thing they agreed on : walking in the snow with snowshoes was a game changer. The distance they walked in one day alone was four times more than what they had walked a couple of days earlier. The first day went by
quickly, and safely, under a beautiful sunshine. Traska spoke
with Mrs. Foxter : she told her about her life in the woods, and why she was there with her friend. Voira told them what direction they needed to take, and when they needed to stop and rest. They stopped to sleep when the wind began to blow. They had a lot of trouble putting up their tents, and

they would never have succeeded without Traska's help. The peaks needed to be buried in the ice, otherwise the tent would have blown away with the wind.

They couldn't see further than six feet away because of the gusts of wind, the snowdrifts and the snow. They eventually managed to finish installing the tents and settling in them. The tents were positioned in such a way that the entrances were face to face, allowing them to communicate with each other. They, ate even though they weren't hungry : they had to force themselves to do so in order to regain strength.

— Tell me, Traska, how much longer is this weather going to be that way?

— All night, and hope tomorrow is okay. But sometimes last several days, nights.

— I hope it won't be the case this time, otherwise we are screwed.

The next day, the wind was as strong as ever, if not stronger. Traska refused to leave because it was too dangerous. And Voira agreed with that wise decision. During the night, Sad and Colmart's tent began to show signs of weakness. And in the middle of the night, the pitons got ripped off by the wind. They had just enough time to move the tools to the other tent, and remove the fasteners that connected this one to it, before it flew away. The five of them squeezed into the remaining tent.

The next day, the wind dropped slightly, enough so that they could break camp and move forward. They were walking slower than before, but they kept a reasonable pace.

— Voira, how far are we from the M3 road?

— Approximately half a day by walk, if, of course, you can keep up with the same pace. The road is behind the woods, that we'll have to cross.

— We're almost out of food.

— Let's settle down on the edge of this wood. Sad and I will go hunting while you pitch the tent.

It was quickly assembled, and the edge of the wood would protect them the wind. They'd been collecting twigs and broken branches to make a fire. Sad and Colmart came back two hours later with a hare.

— That's all we found.

— We'll make do.

Dinner was fairly quick and the only cereal bar they had left was swallowed just as fast. They were on their way back to the tent when a sound of broken twig caught their attention. Colmart whispered to Voira:

— Put the thermal detection system on Albot, please.

Albot's mask immediately switched to thermal mode.

— I'm detecting heat between the trees.

— Animals?

— Animals with two feet, maybe. It looks like there are five of them.

— Put out the fire and the lamps, and get yourselves into nocturnal mode.

Traska didn't quite understand what was going on. But the four friends didn't have time to explain the situation to her.

— Traska, Albot and Mrs. Foxter, go hide behind that snowdrift and don't move. We'll take care of our little visitors. Voira, we're hoping you can help us with this. We're less than them, and I don't think a little help would be too much to ask.

— Where are the five men?

— They are circling us.

— I advise you split up, and move after you shoot. The individuals are right there : one is at 3 o'clock, the other one is at 11 o'clock.

Sad and Colmart aimed their target : they needed to shoot them on their first try, the way they did with the geese last time. That would only leave three men, and rebalance the forces. The silence that reigned was quite impressive. They were all holding their breath, too scared to be seen.

When they put the bullet into the breech, the five men stopped dead. But Sad and Colmart shot right away, thanks to Voira's signal, which didn't give a chance to the two killers.

They immediately responded. The three other killers shot right away in their direction, unloading their assault rifles. But Sad and Colmart had already moved.

The three remaining killers were apparently very upset. They weren't going to have any prisoners. Colmart noticed that the men were communicating in Russian, using military signs.

— They don't look like the guys who chased us in the tunnel and in the hospital. The two we shot were dressed as Russian army figures. That's not normal: something's not right.

— Let's focus on the remaining three. We'll try to understand later.

Two of the three assailants slowed down, taking positions behind the trees. The third one had disappeared.

— Any ideas, Voira?

— Undress completely, and only keep your combinations on.

— I'm sorry, what? Did you lose a processor or something?

— Hurry up, you can't loose any time.

Sad and Colmart foolishly looked at each other and undressed.

— What do we do now?

— I'm going to switch the suits into stealth mode, so they won't be able to see your heat or see you physically. You'll be completely invisible. But you only have three minutes. It consumes a lot of energy. After that, you will become visible again and you'll have to quickly put your clothes back on. The suits will not perform as well because they will only be charged up to 25%.

— Let's go, let's take them down.

— You can't take your guns, just take a knife and put it under your suit.

— Alright, well, let's go. Let's hope the army uniforms they're wearing were only purchased from the scrap army. Because if they're trained soldiers, they're probably going to eat us alive.

— I'll take the one on the left, Sad said.

— And I'll take the one on the right. But I wonder what happened to the third one.

Voira gave them the signal to attack, and which direction to take. Sad and Colmart came in from the sides, unnoticed by the two soldiers. They each took out their knife. They only had one minute left before they would be visible again.

They attacked the two soldiers, almost simultaneously, but their knifes hit a hard material: they were wearing bullet-proof vests. The two soldiers pointed their guns into the void, looking for the source of the attack.

Their suits were going to be visible again, and they were going to get shot on the spot. That's when Voira asked them to strangle the two soldiers. Sad and Colmart were only 20 inches away from their targets when the suits became visible again. They threw themselves on them, and Voira sent an electrical discharge to neutralize them. The two soldiers were now laying on the ground, unconscious.

— What do we do now?

— I personally can't shoot someone in the head while they're unconscious.

— We have to get rid of them, because when they'll wake up they won't hesitate to do the same thing to us.

Once again, Voira gave her opinion, devoid of any feeling and based solely on logic:

— I advise you to kill them now, without thinking about it.

— That's easy for you to say, but I happen to have a soul and a conscious.

— So what do you want to do?

— We tie them to a tree. They'll be able to free themselves. That will give us some time to get out of here.

After tying the two soldiers to a tree, the two friends began to feel the cold reaching their fingertips.

— We have to go get dressed. I'm starting to feel the cold.

— I'm starting to feel it, too. Voira, how much charge do our suits have left?

— Five percent, because I used twenty percent for the electrocution. Get dressed quickly, or you'll freeze.

They came back to get dressed, wondering where the hell the fifth assailant went.

— He may have gone to go get some backup, Sad suggested.

— Maybe, or maybe not?

— Let's go back to the snowdrift.

When they got to the snowdrift, they were completely chocked by what they were witnessing. Blood was coming out of the back of Traska's head. The snow had turned red. Mrs. Foxter was laying unconscious on the ground, and Albot was standing next to a man holding a gun to his head.

— Drop your weapons and get on your knees.

Sad and Colmart were speechless. Their only option was to obey. The killer explained what he wanted:

— Where's the crystal? I won't ask you twice.

— But we don't know where the fucking crystal is!

The killer pointed the gun to Sad's head.

— Take the mask off your suit so I can put a bullet in the skull.

Albot couldn't let another person get killed because of him and that damn crystal. He was going to give it away: he didn't want to hear anything about that thing that had caused so much death around him. That's when Voira intervened:

— Albot, do you have your retractable knife? Don't answer, move your thumb for a yes and pinky for a no.

Albot moved his right hand thumb.

— Alright. You're gonna to stick it into his leg's femoral artery, I'll guide your hand. Are you ready to do this?

Albot moved his little finger to say no.

— We don't have time, in about thirty seconds, this killer is going to shoot Sad. I understand how hard it must be for you to do this. But you don't have a choice!

And she added, as if she had read her mind:

— If you give him the crystal, he'll kill all of you immediately. They will then be able to retrieve the coordinates of the Descendance. And you can only imagine what would happen next.

Albot moved his thumb to signal that he was ready. Sad had removed the hood from his suit, and the killer had his finger on the trigger.

— You can say goodbye to your friend.

Albot took the knife out of his pocket, turned around, and before the killer had time to pull the trigger, he put the knife in the killer's left groin. Normally, the killer's combination would have prevented the blade from piercing him, since the suit was

bulletproof. But Voira had managed to crack the resonance code of the killer's suit, and had sent an opening order to the nanodes.

The enemy was surprised he just got stabbed. A huge squirt of blood gushed from the orifice caused by the blade. The killer immediately understood the severity of the situation. He dropped his gun and started tapping his left forearm, through his jumpsuit. He tried to get away. He was losing a lot of blood, which was supposed to decrease his suit's energy.

Sad and Colmart got their guns back immediately. They would have less scruples about putting a bullet in the head of this one. But the killer, in spite of the pain and the low energy of his suit, found a way to disappear.

Mrs. Foxter slowly came back to her senses. And the four stood there, looking at Traska's lifeless body.

CHAPTER XXII: Recollection and return journey

The four friends were completely discouraged by all these events. They thought all this was a huge injustice. That poor Traska, who didn't ask for anything, or done anything, to deserve such an atrocious death. It was Colmart who broke the silence.

— What's next?
We can't leave that poor girl like that in the middle of nowhere, she'll be eaten by wolves and scavengers.

— She deserves a funeral, added Mrs. Foxter.

— What do you suggest? That we drag her behind us to the next cemetery? We don't even have a shovel to dig a hole. And considering the time of the year, the ground must be hard as concrete.

— As much as it's clear this guy was one of our pursuers, the other four must have been locals. Former soldiers converted in mercenary work. And they didn't just walk here.

— You're right, Sad. They certainly had means of transport. Let's take a look at the other side of the woods.

— Albot and Mrs. Foxter can wait here while we go take a look.

— Take care, gentlemen, don't take any unnecessary risks.
Voira, who had remained silent, appeared.

— We have to think about time, which we're running out of. If we find a mean of transportation, that'll save us a lot of time.
Mrs. Foxter replied:

— As you're constantly learning, take note that humans have a conscience, that often leads them to go against common sense.
Albot couldn't help but add:

— Even though the killers who are after us apparently don't have the shadow of a conscience.

— I can't analyze everything properly, but I'm taking note of it. There's something else I'd like to share with you.

— Yes, Voira!

— Well, if we make it to the airfield, how are we going to pay for your tickets? Moreover, you don't have any documents to travel. A passport or an identity card. Your documents stayed at the base.

— It's true that we left in a bit of a hurry.

The four friends had completely forgotten about that.

— Let's see if we can find the means of transportation that these soldiers used to come here. Then we'll figure it out.

Sad and Colmart walked through the woods, and, after searching for a few minutes, they eventually stumbled upon three snowmobiles, one of which had a fully loaded sled.

— It's strange that this sled is so loaded! They weren't travelling light, it seems.

A gloomy premonition crossed their minds:

— Don't tell me that's Traska's friend's bike?

— If the motorcycle's here, and knowing our killer, they may not have wanted to be burdened by him. Tell me if you see him.

They spent half an hour looking around. They were about to give up their search when Colmart noticed a little red spot on the ground. The snow had almost covered the body.

— Sad, right here! There he is.

A lifeless body was laying on the ground, right in front of them.

— Traska was right to worry.

— I think our pursuers were heading back to the cabin with him. It was the only home close to where we arrived.

— They must have killed him when they saw us. They didn't need him. The body's not in rigor mortis yet.

— Let's put the body on the sled. And let's get back to camp with his snowmobile and one of the two others. Let's hurry and get back to Albot and Helena.

It took them an hour to go around the woods. The path was not very easy and some snowdrifts were in the way. They arrived at the tent, where Mrs. Foxter was starting to worry.

— It took you a while. But apparently it was worth it. You didn't get in any trouble?

— No, but we found Traska's companion.

Sad pointed at the body he had put on the sled.

Mrs. Foxter pouted when she looked at him, and added :

— I've been thinking, and I believe we should go back to the cabin to bury them. Now that we have these bikes, it won't take too long.

— Yes, good idea, it's the least we can do for Traska.

— It's a deal. We'll leave tomorrow at sunrise. The gasoline and the supplies we found on this sled will be useful.

They had a pretty quiet night. And in the early morning, they were all ready.

— Voira! How long do you think it'll take us to get back to Traska's cabin?

— If you leave now, you can be there by noon.

— Let's have a quick lunch, get Traska's body, and go!

— Sad, you take Albot with you on the first bike and I'll take Mrs. Foxter on the second one with the sled.

Within an hour, everything was tidied up and lunch was eaten, thanks to the sleigh which was pretty well stocked.

They arrived around noon, as Voira had planned. The supplies were carried up in the cabin, and put away. It was at least three months' worth of food. They spent the afternoon trying to find a solution for Traska and her companion's grave. Albot suggested they dag in the snow and in the ice under the tree, so they could reach the ground. Then, to use stones to bury them, so the wolves won't come and dig them up.

The longest part was to pick up enough stones. But they had found quite a few near the hot water area, where they had caught the snow geese on Christmas Day. The sleigh, used to transport the stones, made the task much easier.

Traska and her companion were going to be able to rest in peace, side by side. Even though most Russians were Orthodox Christians, they were not sure if that was Traska and her friend's case. So they didn't put any religious sign on the grave, and chose to only engrave Traska and Evan's (they had found his identity papers on him) names on a piece of wood. The four friends prayed for a long time in front of their graves to show their gratitude to the one who had saved them.

Mrs. Foxter suggested they leave first thing in the morning and take the shortest way. The evening meal was rather gloomy and listless. The atmosphere was oppressive. They left the cabin, not without a bittersweet feeling. They left the sled in place and took the strict minimum for the trip.

Albot isolated himself from the others, because he wanted to ask Voira some questions.

— Voira, I just want to check something, to see if I understood your explanation.

— Ask me your question.

— You said we can, how do I put it... We can teleport from one place to another, anywhere we want.

— That works if you give me the right coordinates of your destination, Voira said. To sum it up: the combinations and the nanos that are in your body allows your human structure to withstand it. Otherwise you would be molecularly disintegrated.

— Could you please save the coordinates of this cabin, so that it can only be accessed by me?

— Not a problem, it's already done. Do you have other questions?

— Yes. What's so special about the crystal? And why did my father have it?

— Regarding your father, I don't know. My program was developed to mainly function in the base. But the crystal, it's something else.

— Could you tell me more about it?

— The crystal has two purposes. The first one is to be your memory, and the second one is to serve as an algorithmic vault for the coordinates.

— I don't think I understand your explanations.

— When I say it's your memory, it's because it records everything that happens during your life and can remember your genetic code. And all the places that you visit can be saved in coordinates, just like you did with the cabin. These coordinates, and the algorithm that composes them, must be close to one million digits after the decimal point, which represents a lot of data to be processed and stored. Hence the creation of the quantum computer to process everything, and this kind of memory, based on the same principle as your neurons.

— But how is that possible? What's this cristal made out of?

— It's a graphene derivative. But I don't know its exact composition. What makes this crystal so unique is that it has practically infinite recording possibilities. This is a new technology, which I hardly know anything about.

— You have a different way of talking about us, humans, and about the killers. I don't understand why.

— I'll give you the answers later. Before we leave the base, I was instructed not to say anything about it. There's one thing you have to remember : moving from one point to another is possible, but it requires a lot of energy for the distance. The longer the distance, the more time you'll need to recover.

— What do you mean?

— Well, if we had the coordinates of your destination, which is the Descendance, we could very easily teleport ourselves there. But since it's about four thousand kilometers away from this place, and based on the speed of light which is 983 571 030 feet per second, you would have to wait seventy-five hours before being teleported again. In that case, it's not too serious. But let's say you want to make an intermediate jump. That would make everything much more complicated.

— I think I get it. But since we don't have the coordinates, there's no point in even thinking about it.

Mrs. Foxter had just joined him.

— Are you worried, Albot?

— No, I'm alright. I just needed to talk to Voira to try to understand certain things.

— And did she gave you the answers you wanted?

— Yes, to some questions. But I'm going to wait until I get to the Descendance to ask the other questions.

— I wanted to ask you something, Albot. How are you managing the fact that you're living with Voira, who seamed to have rented an apartment in your brain?

— Let's just say that at first I felt like I was constantly watched. But I'm slowly getting used to it now.

151

— You seem to be taking it pretty well.

— Well, as far as I can remember, I didn't really have a choice.

That last sentence threw an extra layer of cold.

Sad and Colmart joined them.

— What are you two doing?

— We were just talking. Why?

They looked at each other and smiled. They now had a mean of transportation to speed up the journey. But there was still one problem they needed to figure out : the money and the passports. Colmart came up with an idea.

— We could go back to yesterday's little wood and look for our killers. Maybe they had some money in their pockets? That's what we should have done yesterday.

— I don't think that's a good idea. Imagine if they had sent a new group out to look for us.

— What do you suggest?

— We're leaving first thing in the morning, and we'll see what we do when we get there.

Albot came up with an idea:

— I think those two engins must be worth a lot of money. We could sell them once we get there to pay for our tickets. Mr. Colmart would need to be able to contact his superior to deal with the passeports problem.

— That's smart. Let's just get to our destination already, and we'll figure it out.

The journey to Severodvinsk took three days, during which they didn't have any issue. Severodvinsk was founded just before World War II and was then called Soudostroï. During Stalin's greatest communism era, it was a rather modern city, with buildings that were social housings. It wasn't a rich city, and was mainly know for its naval work sites, where most of the Russian nuclear submarines were built. A lot of the Russian troops had settled there, which could explain why soldiers, or former soldiers, could have chased them alongside the killer.

They had some trouble selling the two snowmobiles, but managed to do it. The money they got from it was barely half of their value, but the buyer didn't ask any questions, nor ask for the engine's documents. This was going to allow them to pay for the plane tickets, to book two hotel rooms and buy a hot meal.

But they still had to figure out the passeports issue. They could contact the French embassy, in Moscow, which was thousands of miles away from this town. But that would take far too long, and they would have to give explanations and risk to draw attention to themselves. They had to find another way.

What came to mind was to join Finland, the nearest European country. Once there, they could contact France and ask to be to be repatriated, either on a long flight, or through a UN military base. But they would have to find a way out of Russia. Colmart had asked Sad to go into town with him to try to find a way out of this country.

— There must be smugglers, just like in any other corrupted country.

— I don't think there's any reason why that rule shouldn't apply here, Sad added.

After visiting some of the seediest bars that this place had to offer, and while they were going in the eighth bar, that had once again nothing to offer, they were starting to lose hope. That's when they found themselves face to face with the two killers they disarmed in the woods a few days ago.

CHAPTER XXIII: Remembrance and travel back

The two killers from the woods were as paralyzed and astonished as Sad and Colmart — the only difference was that the two soldiers were armed. Three other soldiers joined the little group and surrounded them. One of the two soldiers spoke to them in Russian. The *Symlium* immediately translated the conversation.

— Is there any good vodka in this bar?

Sad and Colmart felt quite discomfited by the question. They were either pretending now to know them, or they actually didn't recognize them. They couldn't say anything, but raised their shoulders to show that they didn't have the answer to that question. The five soldiers kept walking and entered the bar. They didn't have time to think about it : one of the killers came out of the bar, and asked them in a rather approximative English :

— You alive? You not dead?

Sad and Colmart looked at each other, not knowing what to say. The soldier kept talking:

— Thank you for not killing me. Me not know to kill you.

Colmart didn't know if it was a trap or a chance. If he had wanted to kill them, he could have done it with his buddies earlier, or even now. He had to know for sure:

— You managed to get back here pretty quickly.

— Yes, thanks to the motorcycle left behind by you. Without that, we die of cold.

Sad and Colmart remembered they'd left the third scooter on the spot. The two soldiers must have released themselves quite easily, as planned, and come back with the remaining snowmobile. He was apparently grateful for the chance they had been given.

— We're glad you made it. But who hired you to kill us?

— Him not explain. We kill you, just pay to help him find you.

They understood better now the reasons for his gratitude.

— If me or friend can help you?

They needed to think about the situation.

— We need help, but I need to talk to my friends. Can we meet again tomorrow?

— Possible tomorrow, here nine o'clock?

— Ok, tomorrow, nine o'clock here.

The soldier greeted them and returned into the bar. The two friends didn't know what to think about it. Should they trust people who had tried to kill them a few days before? They went back to the hotel where they were staying, checking behind them, scared they were being followed.

Colmart recounted their evening and the meeting with the two killers they had met and had left alive in the woods.

— That's a crazy story! How can we be sure those two soldiers aren't going to try to kill us?

— If they had intended to do so, I think they would have done it by now. The soldier who spoke to us seemed pretty honest.

— I think we're stuck, we can't escape the country without ID documents. And we're running out of time. We have to get to the Descendance quickly.

— I agree, we're running out of time. We have to get out of this country as soon as possible.

— I don't think we have much choice. We're gonna have to take a risk and ask them for help.

That's when Voira intervened:

— Maybe I can help you.

— How?

— I need Albot to come with you tomorrow, so that I can analyze their behavior and check if they're lying or not.

— Like some kind of lie detector test?

— Kind of, yes. Voice and facial analysis, thermal emissions, neural ripples.

— And that actually works?

— I've never been wrong.

— But if it's a trap, we're handing Albot to them on a silver platter and the crystal as well!

— I think we're stuck, we have to take that risk.
— Well, we'll go armed to that rendez-vous…

The day went by slowly, and they kept taking about the strategy they were going to adopt that same night. Sad wanted to stand back with Mrs. Foxter, with a gun, so he could cover them up, while Colmart wanted to go alone with Sad and leave Albot behind, but close enough so that the killers would be able to talk to him. Voira quickly stopped the discussion: she had to see the soldiers as close as possible, so Albot would need to face the soldiers.
— The four of us will go to that meeting. Let's try to replace our guns with revolvers before tomorrow night.
The guy that had bought the motorcycles did not seem at all surprised to see them again, nor that they wanted to exchange their weapons. They switched the two guns for three revolvers and cartridges. From the look of joy on his face, the buyer thought it was a good deal. Anyway, the rifles were too big and they couldn't walk around town with them. And they surely weren't going to take them on the plane.

They spent the rest of the day hanging around town, wondering if they could trust the soldiers. The evening approached fast, so did nine o'clock.
Our friends made their way to the rendez-vous, not without a certain apprehension. When they arrived, the two soldiers were already on the spot and asked them to come into the bar. They moved to the back of the place and immediately ordered a drink, while introducing themselves:
— My name is Ogor and friend is Priska. Thank you again for not to have killed us.
But our friends, on the other hand, were stunned and didn't introduce themselves in return. These two soldiers were in their twenties at the most, had short hair, shaved cleanly. They weren't wearing a uniform like the day before, therefore had no weapons — at least no weapons they could see. One of the two
soldiers, the one called Priska, looked at them with a less friendly face than Ogor, and added:
— What do you want from us?

— You speak French?

— Me go to college, learn French. So, what do you want?

— We need to get out of this country.

— To go where?

— Finland, since we can't go to France.

— You problem with Russian police? With the army?

— No, we're not in trouble! We're being sued by an organization that wants to kill us, as I'm sure you've noticed.

— Mafia?

— No, and it would take too long to explain, and it wouldn't do any good.

— I'm not even sure you would believe us. Just know that you have nothing to fear from us. We just want to go home.

Voira intervened via the *Symlium*.

— I'm not detecting any anomalies for now. Ask two or three questions, more direct this time, in order to have a better assessment.

Mrs. Foxter, who had remained silent until now, decided to say something:

— To be honest, we don't know if we can trust you. How do we know you're not going to get rid of us outside this bar?

— We not like that. Us take risk too.

— What do you mean?

— We not know you. We not want to kill you. We work for Russian army. They not aware we use army equipment for small business.

— And we have to take your word for it?

Priska stared at them, with a look that spoke volumes about the final exchange.

— Listen. I don't want to help you. Ogor say we live because of you. Then I have to help. But if you don't want, Priska no problem.

He got up and left the table, followed by Ogor. The group took the opportunity to interrogate Voira.

— So, what do you say, Voira?

— My sensors have found nothing that would indicate a danger.

— So we need to bring them back to the table so that we can find a solution.

Sad narrowly caught up with Priska and Ogor, before they passed the bar's front door.

— We trust you. Come. And excuse us for our mistrust, but it's not easy to trust strangers.

Our friends went back to the hotel, puzzled about Priska and Ogor's proposition. Albot wasn't really reassured and wondered whether Voira hadn't made a mistake in her analysis.

— I don't know if I'm the only lucid person here, or if it's because of my young age, but to enter a Russian army base,
get uniforms and travel in one of their planes... I think that it's suicide. If we get caught, we go straight to the gulag.

— Maybe you're right, Albot. But what other option do we have?

— We've already wasted a lot of time. We can't go back home hitch-hiking.

— I know you're right, but still. A military base of the Russian army!

— They're going to get us uniforms that fit us and take care of us in the camp. They're taking as many risks as we are: if they get caught, they'll get executed.

— Well, that's what I don't understand. Why are they helping us if it puts them in danger?

Mrs. Foxter, Sad and Colmart agreed that Albot was right, but they didn't find an immediate solution. Voira intervened :

— Too bad we all don't all have a crystal like Albot.

— Why?

— Well, if it went wrong, I could have send you out from the base. At a known coordinate.

They looked at each other as if Voira had just said something stupid. The same idea had just popped into the heads of the three adults present, and it was Mrs. Foxter who talked about it:

— See, if it goes bad tomorrow night, I want you to take Albot as far away from here as possible.

— The only coordinates I've recorded are the coordinates of Traska's cabin. And I don't think teleporting Albot somewhere else in this town would be a better idea.

— I agree, the military police is probably looking for him everywhere.

— Well, if the cabin is our only option, then take him there.

Albot didn't like what was going on, and the conversation they were all having.

— So what am I supposed to do there? Let myself die slowly? Wait for the killers to find me and put a bullet in my head?

— The important thing is that you get away with the crystal. Voira will help you figure it out.

— How about you?

The question was left unanswered. The time had come, and the four friends went to the rendez-vous spot. The meeting was going to take place in the base, where the nuclear submarines were stored. There was a airport with two runways, which allowed the military equipment, as well as the soldiers, to be transported. Our four friends went into the lion's den.

Priska greeted them in an area located in the southwestern part of the base. He was behind a 20 feet high fence, made out of barbed wire and partly electrified.

— We not waste time. Ogor is going to cut off the power for five minutes. You have to cut the wire fence, pass you and put the fence back. Not a long time.

— Then let's not waste any time.

Priska told Ogor that they were ready. And he proceeded to cut the electric fence. The wire mesh had to be cut in less than one minute so they could enter the base. They were right on time. They were apparently used to conducting this kind of operation. Priska told them to follow him in single file. They
walked a hundred feet in the open without encountering any problems. Eventually, they saw Ogor waving at them to meet him at a door.

— Happy you here, not explode.

— What do you mean, not explode?

— We don't tell you before, but mines are around the base.

Our friends looked at each other and were stunned. They had just walked through a minefield and were in a Russian highly secured military base.

— We come in here and you dress in the clothes I buy.

CHAPTER XXIV: A well-deserved rest

They were inside some kind of big shed where snowmobiles and trucks were put away. Clothes were almost their size, except the ones for Albot, which were a bit too big. Priska gave them time to put on their new outfit.

Colmart had a doubt about Ogor's translation, when they had their conversation in the bar last night.

— You explained to us that there was a flight to one of your bases from Greenland, and that the plane was going to fly over Finland.

— Da.

— And that's where I'm not sure if I got it right. Flying over, it means getting over it! Please reassure us: you meant to stop?

— No. Plane no stop. You jump.

— Excuse me?

Priska showed them four small packages that were attached to a motorcycle. They were parachutes. Mrs. Foxter sat on the floor, white as a sheet.

— Are you out of your mind?

— No, not really. I don't know if I can do that.

— Fully automatic, automatic open parachute. No danger for you.

— I still have to find the courage to jump into the void. Then I'm gonna reach the ground real quick. I'm gonna break a leg. And with the baby, I'm not sure.

— Baby, they shouted. You have baby in belly?

— Yes, two weeks old. And I don't want to lose it.

Our two friends stepped away from the small group and began to discuss loudly. The environment of the warehouse did not allow them to hear the conversation, that was in Russian, very well. But Priska didn't look happy. Ogor was gesticulating, moving around, which didn't feel right.

— What's going on, Priska? Is something wrong?
Our two friends joined them.
— Yes, problem in our heads. We don't want to hurt baby.
— What do you mean, « hurt baby »?
Priska and Ogor were wondering how they were going to be able to explain the situation. It was Priska who spoke:
— We changed parachutes to crush you.
They were completely stunned by what Priska had just said. They couldn't escape without risking to set off a mine. It was a completely grotesque situation. They were shocked.
Albot was right: why would these two soldiers have risked their lives and their careers for complete strangers? How could they have found themselves in that situation? Albot broke the silence, caused by Priska's answer.
— And now you'd rather shoot us right now, or push us onto a mine?
— We don't have a choice. Man return and force us.
— How did he make you do that?
— Man say kill us and family if we don't do it.
— How did he know we were here? And that you were helping us?
— Him have spies everywhere.
— And why did you back out?
— We didn't agree to kill boy (pointing at Albot). And now kill baby.
— And what are you going to do with us?
— You get on plane and go to Finland and jump.
They all looked at each other, wondering if the person they were talking to was trying to fool them.
— After everything you've told us, you really think we can still trust you?
— You choose you. You leave base or you leave plane.
— Give us a few minutes to talk.
— You don't have time, plane leaving. You decide quickly.
Our four friends gathered in the corner of the shed to debate, and try to make a decision.
— So? What do we do?

— Honestly, I don't know what to think anymore. I'm completely lost.

— I think we all are.

Mrs. Foxter still had a problem. She didn't feel like jumping with a parachute. Voira wanted to reassure everyone, but more specifically Mrs. Foxter:

— You mustn't worry too much. I'm supervising your suits. The nanodes will be able to protect the fetus.

— Can they do that?

— And much more. Even if you get hurt, they'll take over.

— Let's not forget that we will surely land on the snow, added Albot.

— The question is whether we can trust our nickel-plated guys or not.

— I think that if they really would have wanted to kill us, they would've already done it. Or they would have thrown us out of the plane.

— Let's go and tell them what we have decided.

Colmart spoke for the group:

— We decided to take the plunge.

— Well, we modify the fall so you get down safe. You no problem now.

Mrs. Foxter was wondering where the hell they were going to land. She had a bad memory of walking in the snow without snowshoes. And she understood that a minimum of survival equipment was required. So she couldn't help but ask:

— We would like to have snowshoes to walk once we arrive, and a tent and some food.

— Um, possible, replied Ogor. Anything else?

— And a satellite phone, Sad added.

— It's hard, needs time. And plane don't wait.

— We have a contact in town who looks like he can get everything. He's not far from here.

— Give address and wait here. See pilot friend plane to wait a little bit.

An hour later, Priska returned, with a happy look on his face.

— Here phone. Him say no traceable and no problem for use.

— Exactly what we need.

Priska and Ogor gave them a crash course on how parachutes worked. It seemed simple to land, but up there, it might be a different story.

— What are we waiting for? Come on, let's go!

Ogor told them goodbye in the warehouse and Priska accompanied them to the plane. Outside, the snow had begun to fall again, and with it came heavy snowfall. You couldn't see further than six feet. Two soldiers, making a round with a dog, approached them. One of the two soldiers spoke to Priska. He, not at all baffled, made a joke in Russian, petted the dog, gave him a sugar he had in his pocket. He offered a cigarette to one of the guards and gave him the pack. The two soldiers started laughing. The dog barked, but without alerting anyone. And they continued their rounds.

The small group made its way to the tarmac where a large transporter was waiting for them. They climbed up the back and Priska tied them to the rather crude passenger seating. And he gave these instructions:

— When red light here is on, you press here to open back plane and jump. Don't forget to take package with equipment
you ask. You turn on the light on parachute to see you and package.

— Thank you, Priska. Thank you for everything.

— How are you going to deal with the person who asked you to make us disappear?

— I say you discover in plane problem parachute. Or me tell I don't understand problem.

He smiled and winked at Mrs. Foxter. He added:

— You good luck, and me when I visit Paris, you pay vodka to Priska and Ogor.

— Not a glass, but a bottle, Colmart added.

The four engines of the Russian carrier started up, and filled the cabin with a noise that prevented any audible dialogue. Albot asked anyway:

— How long before the red light comes on?

— About two hours. You can sleep.

He greeted everyone and left the transporter by pressing the big green button that closed the back door.

The two hours went by faster than they would have liked. Sad had been in the army, and had already jumped out of a plane. Colmart, on the other hand, only did a parachute jump once and didn't have a very good memory of it. As for Mrs. Foxter and Albot, it was going to be their first time. And they didn't feel very well.

Voira asked them to wear hoods and gloves, in order to see and be seen in the dark, and avoid the cold when they're up in the air. The flashing light came on, with a sound indicating that it was time to go. They weren't were enthusiastic, but they knew they'd gone too far to change their mind. Colmart pressed the button to open the door, letting the wind in, with a deafening noise.

— Sad, throw the package, and jump. Albot and Helena, you will go next, and I will go last.

They jumped, not without some apprehension that the parachute would not open once they hit the ground, which made the descent interminable. But a thousand feet high, all four parachutes opened. The four friends and the package all landed within a radius of approximately five hundred yards. The light attached to the parachutes was easily visible at night, which allowed them to get their bearings and gather fairly quickly.

They retrieved the package with the gear and got equipped with the snowshoes. Then, they took out the flashlights and a map of Finland Ogor had given them.

— Apparently, I didn't break anything, Colmart said.

— No, all the sensors are green, Voira said.

— Great, which way do we go?

— We need to walk towards the nearest town.

— According to the coordinates I'm reading, we're not too far from a town called Hollola.

— How many miles away is it?

— About 30.

— But we're still wearing Russian uniforms. We can't walk around like this.

— Our clothes are in the package.

— It's a good thing we have our suits. Because getting undressed with these negative temperatures would have been challenging.

After putting on their clothes and burying the uniforms and the parachutes in the snow, our friends started walking. A halo of light started to appear in the distance, a good hour after their departure.

— We're not far away.

— Another little hour, I think, said Voira.

They arrived on a road with very little traffic, where hitch-hiking didn't seem to be a common habit. But who would've taken four people at night and in the middle of nowhere? So they had no other option but to keep going with their snowshoes. Mrs. Foxter was feeling tired.

— I would give anything for a warm bed and a hot meal.

— We still have quite a few dollars left from our snowmobile transaction. It's a good thing we asked for dollars instead of rubles.

— I hope we'll find a hotel quickly.

After wandering around the city for over an hour, they finally saw a cottage looking hotel. This one was practically empty, and the person at the reception asked them which cottage they would like to stay in. The rental was worth a pittance in this season. Our friends had no papers on them, and wondered if this was going to be a problem. But the hostess gave them the key without asking any questions. The mentality of the people in northern Europe really had nothing to do with the population of central Europe. The young woman explained that it was too late for her to prepare a meal for them, but that there was a gas station across the street that served the entire night.
The travelers were tired, but they were also very hungry. The hostess walked them to the cottage and showed them around. It was some sort of two-story wooden house, which was usually rented to families during the holidays. There were three bedrooms, two of which were upstairs, two bathrooms, a kitchen and even a sauna. Our friends quickly settled down and went out to have dinner.

There were two other people in the gas station, that must have been truck drivers. The gas station attendant, who was also the waiter and the cook, told them, in perfect English, that at this time of day, the choices on the menu were quite limited. Everyone had the reflex to look at the two truck drivers' dishes.

— Same as them, It'll be fine, ordered Mrs. Foxter.

They took advantage of the wait to assess the situation.

— It's late, maybe we should get some rest, Sad suggested.

— You're right, I'm exhausted. Let's sleep on it, replied Mrs Foxter. A shower and a nice bed, that's all I need right now. We'll make a decision tomorrow morning at breakfast.

— And let's not forget that we have the satellite phone, added Colmart. Tomorrow we'll call my boss and have him find us a solution to go back to France.

Once the meal was over, the group left the gas station. The snow was starting to fall heavily.

— It's a good thing the snow is only starting to fall now and not when we jumped out of the plane. We would have had a hard time to gather and walk.

— We're lucky, for once!

And they went into the cottage.

CHAPTER XXV: Early Departure

They had a good night sleep, and they only woke up around noon the next morning. They were starving, and their bellies were screaming with hunger. The hostess greeted them with the same broad smile as the night before, and offered them a traditional Finnish lunch. They didn't know much about Finnish cuisine.

Colmart would have preferred a big, rare steak with very oily fries and a good glass of wine. But he didn't say anything, perhaps to avoid Mrs. Foxter's unpleasant comments and remarks about his diet.

The menu on the table was written in Finnish, and the photos of the dishes weren't very appetizing. Colmart eventually called the waitress, who was speaking in a pretty rough English, which was pretty surprising for someone living in this country. The waitress tried her best to translate the menu, but they still couldn't understand anything.

What they had understood thanks to Voira's translation was that they had some kind of Baltic herring gratin or, alternatively, reindeer, a thick pancake baked in the oven, and bread called « setuuri ». For dessert, they had a cake called « bostonkakku », and, as for drinks, she offered them « glövi », that looked like hot fruity wine.

The very good quality meal was served and swallowed quite quickly. The guests felt full and rested.

— So, what do we do now?, Sad asked again.

— I'm going to call our supervisor to see how he can get us out of here, Colmart replied.

— We're gonna waste too much time, I'm gonna call someone above so we can figure it out faster.

— Oh, yes, I forgot you had your special favors, Mrs. Foxter.

— I don't think it's a good time to be sensitive, Colmart. We must go as quickly as possible to the Descendance. Before it's too late. There are a lot of people's lives at stake.

— I'm sorry, you're right.

Colmart took the phone out of his pocket and handed it to Mrs. Foxter:

— I'll leave you to it, then.

The phone was pretty big, with a huge antenna that unfolded, but it wasn't nearly as rudimentary as they might have imagined. Apparently, that wouldn't be the last surprise they would have to face with that Russian seller. He couldn't have been that dishonest.

Mrs. Foxter stepped away from the table to dial the number of her government contact. The discussion lasted a good fifteen minutes. When she returned to her seat, her face wasn't sending a positive signal.

— What's going on? You look like someone who just got some bad news. Has there been a new eruption of the Eyjaf something volcano? I can never say it right.

Mrs. Foxter painfully smiled.

— You mean Eyjafjallajökull, I suppose?

— Yes, that's it. Bless you.

She preferred not to outbid the joke, because the news that her contact had brought to her made her feel sick.

— They're sending a helicopter to pick us up tonight. There's a UN base not far from Helsinki.

— There a UN military base in Finland?

— Apparently, yes.

— Well? That's just great! Why the sad face?

— We're wanted for kidnapping, murder, and bomb attack.

Sad, Colmart and Albot were stunned. The waitress, who had come to get the empty plates, was surprised by their faces as well.

— What do you mean, wanted?

— Our disappearance from the hospital is consistent with the explosions that have taken place at the same time around the facility. And the media are probably being manipulated, they said everything was our doing.

— And what abductions and murders are they talking about?

— Albot's abduction and the murder of a hospital guard who was in charge of video surveillance. A second one is in a coma.

— But that's a load of crap! And no one took our defense?

— According to the media, you're two dirty cops who allegedly kidnapped Albot to get the technology his dead father gave him. And I am a spy for a foreign power.

— Great, we're wanted by Interpol, I guess?

Albot had said those empty words. But the silence that followed made him uncomfortable.

— No, but really? Are we wanted by Interpol?

— If that's the case, the UN will never get us out of this. I think we'll get a visit from the police of the equivalent of the French GIGN.

— What do you want to do? Wait for them to come and get us tonight?

— Or shoot us down, Albot ended.

Our friends felt like they were falling from the Charybdis into Scylla. They now understood why Mrs. Foxter's had that sad look on her face. Colmart wanted to know the details:

— Mrs. Foxter, is your contact trustworthy?

— I would trust him with my life.

Then why would he inform you of everything we're accused of and then tell you that he's going to have us evacuated by the UN? This is nonsense! Or maybe that's the message he wanted us to get. He probably feels watched or bugged. And couldn't speak freely.

— A message to say what?

— Something like: « run away », said Albot, to once again close the conversation.

Colmart had come to the same conclusion: they had to leave as soon as possible. They now knew their location, and he didn't think they were going to wait until evening to come get them.

— We need to get out of here fast.

— We need to find a means of transportation without drawing anyone's attention.

— There's probably a rental car company around here somewhere.

— And how can you rent a vehicle without any identification or credit card?

— You're too defeatist, Colmart joked.

— And you are too unconscious, replied Mrs. Foxter. Let's stop the squabble and think of a solution.

— We could try to get hitch-hiked by one of those truck drivers?

— You, as a truck driver, would take two guys, a woman and a teenager in your truck?

— When you put it like that, I don't think so.

— There wouldn't be enough room anyway.

— Let's see if we can find a rental car company in this town. There must be one, right?

After a short half-hour search in downtown and in the surroundings, they still couldn't find any rental car companies, but they ended up seeing a car dealership.

— Damn, it's closed for the holidays. It will only reopen next week.

— You thought you'd be able to buy one with the two hundred bucks we have left?

They looked at each other, and this time they couldn't help but smile.

— But it's even better, Albot exclaimed.

— What do you mean?

— We steel a car so that there won't be any trace. And I don't think he's afraid of having anything stolen from him. He probably doesn't even have an alarm in the store.

— I wouldn't be so sure. But I'm still going to do what needs to be done. I'm going to cut off the phone feed in case there's a remote alarm.

Sad walked around the building, trying to find the telecom feed. After a good ten minutes, he ended up coming across a white box with a phone drawn on it. He opened it up and ripped out the wires of telecom arrivals.

The fugitives also easily found a way to get into the shop. One of the back doors had a simple lock. Colmart, which had followed a particular training in the police, opened it within a couple of seconds. Once inside, and

after looking around for a few minutes, they found the car keys and the cars'
papers in a drawer.

— What should we take, Sad asked.

— Maybe a 4x4 car, because of the snowy roads, Colmart replied.

— And which direction are we taking?

— Helsinki, replied Mrs. Foxter. But first, let's go back to the
cottage to get our stuff back.

The car dealer was only three blocks away from their cottage. Our
friends got there in less than five minutes. Sad, who was driving the car,
volunteered to fill up the gas tank while Colmart would pay the bill, and Mrs.
Foxter and Albot would go and get their stuff.

— I'll fill up the tank and pick you up in front of the cottage. And
don't dawdle on the way.

Everyone went in the direction they were meant to go. Colmart
entered the reception and pressed the little bell on the counter to call the
hostess. He waited a good minute, but no one came. He couldn't wait for
ever, they had to leave this place as soon as possible. After ringing the bell
twice more and waiting twice as long, he checked the price chart. He left the
necessary amount, added a small tip, and a little note with the number of the
cottage.

As he left the reception, he was greeted by a strong wind and by the
snow, which had started to fall. A lighter wind, however, than the one that
had blown up their tent the other night. While recalling that episode, he
remembered Traska's horrible death. How could human beings kill others
for no reason at all? He really would never understand human nature.

He was only 20 feet away from the cottage when he saw shadows
at the window. He kept moving forward in the snow, which was getting
heavier with every step he took. He was lost in thoughts when he stopped
dead. There were shadows, too many for them to be just Albot, Sad and
Colmart's. Something wasn't right.

He walked around the cottage and approached the kitchen window.
And what he saw made him freeze. Albot and Mrs. Foxter were sitting on
the couch with the hostess, who was turning her back to the fireplace. One
of the two men was looking out the window that was near the front door.
And the second one was pointing his gun at Albot. They were probably

waiting for them. Colmart had left the gun he bought in Russia in his room. Aside from sending snowballs, he's didn't really know what to do.

Voira, who had remained silent until then, contacted Colmart.

— Can you hear me, Mr. Colmart?

— Yes, Voira! I'm standing by the kitchen window, I see what's going on. Any ideas on how to get you out of there?

— Not for now, but we're running out of time.

— I have an idea. Ask Albot to go to the toilet so that he can open the window for me.

— And then what?

— Let me in. And I'll figure it out.

Albot, just like Mrs. Foxter, had been listening to the discussion between Voira and Colmart.

— Sir, could I go to the bathroom, he asked.

The nearest killer looked at him dismissively and said no with his head. Albot insisted several times but the killer didn't want to hear anything about it. Too bad for Colmart.

— But what do they want, Colmart asked Voira.

— They are waiting for a group to join them. And by the time it gets here, it'll be too late.

— Are those our killers?

— Apparently not. They want all four of you alive.

— That's news to me!

— I don't think these are your usual pursuers. These ones don't have suits. I can't figure out who they are. What about Sad, where is he?

— He came by to pick up our stuff and load it in the car. And he's waiting for us at the gas pump. He wanted to take a road map and something else.

— I may have a solution, but there is a risk, explained Voira.

— Please explain, Voira, and connect us all so that we can hear you.

Colmart met Sad at the gas station, who was pacing back and forth in front of the car

— I was starting to get worried. Where are the other two?

Colmart explained to Sad the situation.

— Shit, and you think that's gonna work?

— Voira thinks so, but she's not a hundred percent sure. It has never been tempted before. She thinks so, specially after your little adventure in the tunnel with the master. Let's get ready to leave as soon as they arrive.

— Where are you going?

— I'm gonna check something in the diner.

Sad got behind the staring wheel, started the car and got it ready to go. Colmart walked into the gas station and looked over at the table where they had dinner the night before. Two truck drivers were having dinner at that same table, where

Sad and Colmart had once sat. That's when Mrs. Foxter and Albot appeared sitting next to the two truck drivers. They almost had a Cardiac arrest! And the waitress knocked over her coffee pot full of coffee. If they could tell this misadventure to anyone who wanted to hear it, who'd be likely to believe them?

They leaned against the wall as if the two new people were ghosts. Our three friends got out of the gas station as fast as

possible. Their legs were wobbly, but Mrs. Foxter and Albot were still alive. They collapsed in the back of the car without saying a word.

— Drive, Sad! Step on the gas!

The car sped away, in a slight sliding motion due to the snow.

— Well done, Voira, but you're gonna have to explain.

CHAPTER XXVI: Return journey

The road to Helsinki was white, and the snowplow hadn't done its job yet. The group soon slowed down, to match with the country's limitations and therefore not draw attention to themselves. Moreover, riding on slippery snow wasn't really Sad nor Colmart's hidden talent.

Colmart ended up asking Voira about that famous miracle:

— When I said that this was the first time this kind of portering had ever been done, I meant it. Although the term « meant » may not be the most appropriate for a machine. Usually, it is impossible to carry two people simultaneously. You have to rely on a huge amount of energy to do that kind of operation. But since I realized that the distance was less than a mile, I thought it might just work. Even if it meant that Albot's suit energy will be drastically lowered.

— Is that why he collapsed as soon as he got on board, and why he's still asleep?

— Without a doubt, yes. For him, this is the equivalent of a thousand miles journey, in terms of portage. His combination would have been unable to support that load without the crystal. As I am part of him, I was able to model the equation in order to transfer two individuals. I'm only now starting to enter the logarithm of the crystal. But only from time to time, as if it was capable of self-analysing itself.

— And what would have happened if you had been wrong? Or if the place or the space was already busy?

— If the space is occupied by a natural material, an object, or by a human being, the outcome is usually death. We then would have witnessed an instant molecular fusion. But during the transfer, I was able to make a projection of a few attoseconds.

— « Attoseconds »? What the hell is that?

— It's the quantum unit of measurement. As I've already explained to you in the base, I'm a quantum computer. As I was saying, when I made the transfer, my projection was about five attoseconds ahead of schedule.

— And what does being the speed champion at the Olympics Games get you?

— I assume that's human humor? To answer your question, that would make it possible to shift in the arrival space, in order to avoid molecular fusion. Or, if I push my logic, to perform a quantum pre-portation, before proceeding to the actual portation. And to avoid any death.

— That's great! But I guess there's an « if »?

— Exactly! The person must have a quantum computer in his or her brain, as well as a crystal, just like Albot.

— Two things that make Albot unique, Sad said.

— Don't tell him that when he wakes up, or he'll get big-headed, added Colmar

Voira had finished her technology monologue, and wondered if these humans had the ability to understand her explanation.

— I didn't quite understand everything, Colmart admitted. And you, Sad, don't pretend like you have it all figured it

— To be completely honest with you, I've stopped listening pretty quickly. I need some aspirin. Is there a *For Dummies* book on that topic?

— How about you, Mrs. Foxter?

But Mrs. Foxter, who had listened to Voira's explanation, had fallen asleep, with her head quite full.

The two-hour drive to Helsinki went by quickly. Halfway there, they had been overflown by two large helicopters and had drove passed several police vehicles. They were right to leave.

After dropping off the car in the airport parking lot, they walked towards the check-in counters.

— I don't understand what we're doing here, Albot. You asked to come here, but I still don't understand why.

— We don't have enough money to take four tickets, and no identification documents to get through customs. Voira has an idea, but she needs to try something first. We need to find a place where we will be able to access the airport's Internet. It's perfect here: we sit down and quietly have a coffee with a delicious Finnish pastry.

— You seem to be taking this rather lightly, Albot?

— Let's just say that I'm starting to get a better grasp of some things, and to get used to Voira.

— What do you mean?

— Well, in the car, while I was asleep, my brain got connected to a part of Voira. She asked my permission, because that might have ended up injuring or destroying part of my brain.

— But you're crazy, boy!

— I have to live with it, so I might as well get used to it. And the result is that I'm now able to communicate with her live, without even talking. It's not perfect yet, because I still have to focus a lot and it gives me strong headaches.

— And what do you want to do?

— With no papers and no money, all there's left is hacking. And with a quantum computer on our side, why not take advantage of it? Just relax, and I'll explain everything in a few minutes. I don't want to get your hopes up.

An hour flew by, and the four friends waited patiently for Voira's verdict. This time, she spoke by herself, without using Albot's voice.

— I've managed to get through their various security fences. I chartered a private jet to take us to the Toulouse-Blagnac airport.

— Whose jet is it? Aren't they going to notice?

— This is the jet of a self-centered American billionaire who arrived yesterday and is leaving after the holidays. I have prepared and transmitted the flight plan to the pilot and air traffic controllers. There's a stewardess that will pick you up at gate seven, at 11 P.M. She'll take us directly to the plane on the tarmac, without going through the whole usual process. Not to mention you still have your weapons!

— Damn, we completely forgot to get rid of them.

— Maybe it's not so bad we have them. We haven't reached our destination yet.

— How should we introduce ourselves to the hostess? We have to give her a document or an identification of some sort, right?

— The good thing about billionaires is that some of them are just so full of themselves they just can't stand it to justify themselves, especially when the plane belongs to them. And according to the Internet, the billionaire whose jet we're borrowing is in that category. He is even depicted as someone who doesn't talk to mere mortals. He thinks he's above the law and doesn't like to justify his choices nor actions. I don't think the hostess and the pilot are going to be very talkative. They've been given instructions and they're being paid to transport them, not be friendly.

The four friends were only half convinced by Voira's small speech, but they were hoping she made the right choice, otherwise they'd all end up sleeping in jail.

They had boarded the jet and were now comfortably seated. They couldn't believe it. Was their luck finally switching?

— Well, Voira, you bluffed me.

— I can't believe we're finally going to be able to go home!

The hostess had indeed been there, waiting for them at gate seven. She did not ask any questions and took them straight to the jet, thanks to her badge. She was probably used to working for one of those billionaires that couldn't stand talking to the staff.

It was one of the latest Dassault Falcon jet. They boarded the ship, not without hesitation. But once inside, they were all
amazed by so much luxury. It would have been hard to be picky, with the immaculate white leather seats and the lacquered wooden tables. They were all amazed.

The captain informed them that the flight would last approximately four hours, and that snacks were available. The hostess brought a meal and did everything she could to fulfill every single one of their wishes during the flight.

Everyone fell asleep. Lulled by the humming of the plane, they finally felt safe. There was nothing like living the life of a billionaire. They thanked the captain and the hostess for the excellent trip they'd made.

And surprise! No welcoming committee was waiting for them when they came down the airplane. The stewardess took them to the exit door, so they wouldn't be bothered by anyone.

— It feels good to have a normal trip, without getting shot, without being teleported, without any parachute jumping.

Sad, Colmart and Mrs. Foxter couldn't help but smile at Albot's joke.

— Now we need to find a vehicle so that we can join the Descendance.

— Is it far from the airport, Mrs. Foxter?, Albot asked.

— About two short hours away.

They were exhausted by all their adventures and haunted by the deaths they witnessed. The only thing they wanted was for it all to end. And the Descendance was the best destination for them. They wanted to think that, once they would get there, they would be safe, as if that nothing could ever hurt them again. At least for a while. They needed to recharge their batteries, to regain strength, to be able to sleep soundly, without being constantly on the look-out.

That's when Mrs. Foxter recognized Pierre Dulmon, who was the head of the stewardship at the Descendance.

— Pierre! What are you doing here?

— Helena! How nice to see you safe and sound. What was broadcasted on the news made you look like an industrial spy. Some sort of 21st century Mata Hari. They kissed like old friends who hadn't seen each other for a long time. And Pierre explained why he was at the airport:

— I'm here to pick up three new teens who are joining our community. They were supposed to arrive last night, but due to a last minute hitch, the trip was postponed.

— Aren't you going to introduce me to your friends?

— Yes, of course. This is Detective Colmart and his deputy, Officer Sad. And this young man is Jonathan and Orlea Coldi's son.

— No way? Is it Albot? My sincere condolences, my boy, for the disappearance of your parents and your sister.

— Thank you, sir.

Albot felt like that occurred such a long time ago. The airport's speakers spat out a barely audible message, directed to Mr. Pierre Dulmon: the three children he was supposed to pick up were waiting for him at gate two.

— Wait for me here, I'll be back in two minutes. I came with the minivan. We can travel together and you can me tell your story on the way.

Mrs. Foxter, however, didn't really want to get into details. Especially since Pierre was a nice guy, but a real blabbermouth. If by some misfortune she were to tell him all the things that had happened, she was certain that even the Martians would be informed the very next day.

She limited the explanations to the bare minimum, and hid herself behind the need to talk to Director Ziegler first. Pierre understood, and immediately stopped talking about it.

The minivan was spacious enough to accommodate eight people. The journey to the Descendance seemed to take an eternity. And the three teenagers Pierre had picked up hadn't spoke for the whole trip. They hadn't introduced themselves, and they weren't polite enough to even say hello. Apparently, they weren't really happy about going to live at the Descendance.

After going through a fairly dense forest, they began climbing a hill. The Descendance was at the very top of that hill, which was overlooking a huge cliff. The main entrance looked like a castle with its drawbridge over a huge pit. They
crossed this drawbridge, followed by the huge gate that opened onto a courtyard.

Once the vehicle stopped, the passengers got out, one after the other. Mrs. Foxter came out last. An old gentleman came to greet them.

— Helena, how is that possible?

— Mr. Ziegler. How nice to see you again.

It was then that two men appeared in the courtyard, about ten yards away, pointing their weapons in their direction. Sad rushed towards them, hoping he could intercept the bullet before it hit Albot. And without saying a word, one of the two men pulled the trigger. Sad collapsed immediately. Albot thought:

— We're too late.

PROLOGUE 8

CHAPTER I : The accident..10

CHAPTER II : All alone 13

CHAPTER III : The awakening 17

CHAPTER IV : The cylinder...23

CHAPTER V: Home sweet Home..27

CHAPTER VI: Descent History 33

CHAPTER VII: The Crystal...40

CHAPTER VIII: Hide and seek 47

CHAPTER IX: The Attack 52

CHAPTER X: The extraction...59

CHAPTER XI: The hunt 67

CHAPTER XII: The Tunnel 74

CHAPTER XIII: The rescue 82

CHAPTER XIV: The Door...88

CHAPTER XV: The Basics 95

CHAPTER XVI: Non-Cartesian Choices............................102

CHAPTER XVII: Last Wishes 109

CHAPTER XVIII: The Passage..116

CHAPTER XIX: The Pack..123

CHAPTER XX: Christmas in the woods 131

CHAPTER XXI: The ambush..139

CHAPTER XXII: Recollection and return journey 147

CHAPTER XXIII: Remembrance and travel back................154

CHAPTER XXIV: A well-deserved rest..................................161

CHAPTER XXV: Early Departure 168

CHAPTER XXVI: Return journey 175